"Who was that guy? Are you lovers?"

"Al?" She smiled against his skin. "No—we're friends."

Fletch faced her suddenly. "And why should I believe that?"

Jolian touched his cheek. "Because I say it."

His smile vanished into a wary blankness. "I lived with a wife for seven years," Fletch said carefully, "who claimed she loved me. And all the while she was sleeping with anyone who asked. So why should I believe *you*?"

"Because I'm me," Jolian whispered. "And I *do* love you."

His neck muscles jerked and went rigid beneath her hand. "Don't do this to me," he growled, jaws clenching. "I hurt just looking at you."

"Good," she murmured. She wanted him to hurt. Any way to reach him was better than no way at all. She snuggled against his shoulder, wondering if ice hurt when it melted. "Good," she whispered, and slept.

Books by Peggy Nicholson

HARLEQUIN PRESENTS
732—THE DARLING JADE
741—RUN SO FAR

These books may be available at your local bookseller.

For a list of all titles currently available,
send your name and address to:

Harlequin Reader Service
P.O. Box 52040, Phoenix, AZ 85072-2040
Canadian address: P.O. Box 2800, Postal Station A,
5170 Yonge St., Willowdale, Ont. M2N 5T5

PEGGY NICHOLSON

run so far

Harlequin Books

TORONTO • NEW YORK • LONDON
AMSTERDAM • PARIS • SYDNEY • HAMBURG
STOCKHOLM • ATHENS • TOKYO • MILAN

Harlequin Presents first edition November 1984
ISBN 0-373-10741-2

Original hardcover edition published in 1984
by Mills & Boon Limited

CHAPTER ONE

'A VEGETARIAN *rugby* player? Now I *know* you're lying!' Laughing, Jolian shook her head as the phone rang. 'Oops!'

'I'm not, he is, and it's your turn!' Katy announced, sliding off the edge of her friend's desk. She skipped around the tall filing cabinets which split the room into two offices, and disappeared.

Taking a deep breath to banish all laughter from her voice, Jolian picked up the phone. It was important not to sound too cheerful. Sympathetic—yes; obnoxiously happy—no. 'Reachout Hotline,' she said quietly. 'Can I help you?'

'Er ...' It was a girl's voice, soft with uncertainty. Jolian swallowed audibly. 'Hi, I ...' The tiny voice trailed away again and the girl sighed, a small, breathy sound of despair.

She's going to hang up, Jolian thought anxiously, squeezing the receiver. 'My name's Jolian,' she offered quickly. 'What's yours?' If she could just start the kid talking.

'Er ... Suzie,' the girl sighed again.

'Hi, Suzie. How's it going?' Jolian leaned slowly back in the swivel chair, her long legs stretched out before her. Dark blue eyes gazed up at the peeling paint on the ceiling above her and stared right through it, picturing instead the scared child who went with the voice. 'You doin' okay?'

'Er ... I don't know.' The soft voice was squeaky, now with swallowed sobs. 'I thought so ... but now ...' She sniffed faintly.

'When did you run away?' Jolian coaxed, hoping it

5

was recently. The kid certainly didn't sound street-toughened yet. Not that it took long. Sometimes the runaways found out within hours that they'd jumped from the frying pan into the fire. Sometimes they found out too late ... She shut her eyes and frowned, this was no time to be thinking of Jane.

'It was ... I guess it was Sunday. Mom and I had an awful f-f-fight.' Quavers turned to sobs and then were muffled as if Suzie covered the mouthpiece with a hand.

Jolian waited a moment. 'Do you want to go home again, Suzie?' she asked finally. 'Try to make it up?'

'I *can't*! They won't want me now! I ...' Her voice shuddered and broke upwards and she muffled the phone again.

Jolian shook her head and waited, half smiling. Sometimes that was true, the parents didn't want the kids back. Many of the runaways fled homes racked by poverty, by divorce, alcoholism, or other, even worse, problems. Their parents were too exhausted, too bitter, too disturbed to have any love to spare for their own children. But other youngsters struck out on their own in momentary defiance or despair, or out of sheer stubborn teenage pigheadedness, leaving behind families who would miss and mourn them. Somehow she thought that might be Suzie's case. 'Want me to call them for you and see if that's true, Suzie? I bet your mother's sitting by the phone right now, waiting.'

There was the quick sound of indrawn, hopeful breath, then slowly she let it out again. 'But I *can't* go home yet, I've got to pay Tony back first ...'

Jolian felt the hairs at the nape of her neck stir. 'Tony?' she asked casually. 'Who's Tony, Suzie?'

'My ... my new boyfriend ...' It was a statement, but the last word rose uncertainly as if there were some question to it.

'Where'd you meet him, Suzie?'

'At the bus station, the first night. He's been taking

care of me. He's . . . spent a lot of money on me.' Once
more there was the questioning lilt to her voice. It was
the first stirring of adult wariness. Getting something
for nothing was a child's dream.

Jolian sighed. So it wasn't going to be so easy after
all. 'And what do you have to do, to pay him back,
Suzie?' she asked, knowing the answer all too well
already.

But Suzie hadn't guessed yet, or couldn't admit it to
herself if she had. 'He won't say. I've got to work for
him, but he hasn't said where yet . . .'

On the streets is where, you poor little chump! Jolian
gritted her teeth to keep the words in. 'Look, Suzie,
when will he be . . .'

'*Hey!* Who ya talkin' to?' A distant crash followed
that slurred yell—a door banging open?—and the girl
squeaked.

'*Gimme* that!' Jolian flinched as hand met flesh in a
resounding smack at the other end of the phone line
and the girl cried out again. The phone fell clattering to
the floor.

Suddenly a hoarse breath rasped in Jolian's ear and
she shuddered violently. The pimp was listening now. If
she could just cover for Suzie somehow. She swallowed
hard and spoke. 'That's two pizzas—large—mushrooms, mozzarella, peperoni, cut the anchovies,' she
gabbled nasally. 'Ya wanna pick these up or ya wan'em
delivered?'

'*Pizza?*' Outrage struggled with confusion in the
coarse voice. 'Pizza, my——' the phone slammed down,
cutting off the obscenity, and Jolian threw back her
head and whooped.

She looked up to find Katy goggling at her from the
file cabinets and she laughed again, leaning back in her
chair and waving the receiver helplessly. 'C-cut the
anchovies!' she chortled as Katy took the phone and
hung it up for her, shaking her head. Shivering with

reaction, Jolian folded her legs up into the swivel chair and gave it a spin. The buildings and traffic of Kenmore Square, Boston, rotated into view and then disappeared as she twirled past the windows and back towards Katy again. Her short, stocky friend was scowling at her as she spun by.

'Jolian, would you calm down and tell me what's so funny!'

'Nothing is!' Jolian grabbed the edge of her desk and jerked to a halt, her grin fading suddenly. Hugging her knees, she stared up at her friend, her thick, dark brown hair fanned out over her shoulders. 'I was talking with a kid who's been picked up by a pimp. He walked in right as I was getting through to her.' She shivered. 'He's probably beating the living daylights out of her this minute, if I didn't fool him with my pizza brainstorm!' Her arms tightened around her knees as she shuddered again.

'Or maybe it sounded like a super idea, and he's taking her out for a peperoni special right now,' Katy soothed. She was a nurse with a cheerful, practical outlook on life. They made a good hotline team, her steady temperament balancing Jolian's mercurial moods. 'Some pimps control their girls by being nice to them, you know.'

'Mmm, I suppose so.' Jolian frowned, her dark, winged brows flattening into a straight line above deep-set eyes. 'But he didn't sound like the nice type, Katy. He sounded like a bully boy.' She sighed.

Katy eased a trim, blue-jeaned hip on to the battered desktop. 'Jolian, you win some, you lose some, and some you get rained out. You know the statistics. More than half a million kids run away from home every year.' She smiled down at her friend. 'You'll get a chance to help a few of 'em.'

'Mmm, I know.' Jolian untangled her legs and sat up, reaching for one of the needle files on the desktop. 'But

I wanted to help that one,' she muttered, staring down at the tool. Picked up by a pimp—was that what had happened to Jane, so long ago?

'Well, now she knows we're here, maybe she'll call back again when she gets a chance,' Katy said briskly, standing up. The phone rang. 'My turn,' she announced sternly as Jolian reached for it. She dashed between the file cabinets and back to her own desk. 'Reachout Hotline . . .'

'And some you get rained out,' Jolian whispered ruefully. She set the file down and picked up the thick piece of sterling silver she'd been smoothing earlier. Some day soon it would be a bracelet. Restlessly she put it down again and stood up, stretching her slender, athletic frame to its full five feet five inches. People always guessed she was taller. It was her thinness, or something in the eager, long-legged way she moved, which deceived them.

Half listening to Katy's encouraging murmurs from the other side of the room, Jolian drifted across the small office, ending up at the makeshift cooking counter with its hotplate and coffeemaker. Coffee . . . she checked her watch and then shrugged. Why not? Digging a quarter out of the pocket of her shorts, she dropped it in the dish on the counter. She had half an hour to go before her shift was finished.

Leaning back against the counter, she sipped from her mug and studied the shabby room, its dusty bay windows glowing now with the sinking sun's rays, its filing cabinets filled with the names of the missing, the seeking, and the names of the found, the cot in the corner where she'd caught many a catnap these last five years, and the one object of vital, overwhelming importance—the phone on her ancient sunlit desk. For that was what Reachout Hotline was—a phone line, open twenty-four hours a day, every day of the year.

The phone rang. It was the local line again, Jolian

noted as she crossed the room; Katy was still talking on one of the two toll-free long-distance lines. 'Reachout Hotline,' she said pleasantly, 'can I help you?'

'Er . . . I hope so.' It was a boy's voice this time, gruff with the effort to sound like a man.

She found herself smiling and was glad he couldn't see her face. 'My name's Jolian Michaels,' she said gravely. 'What can I do for you?'

'I'm pleased to meet you, Jolian,' the boy said formally. In an adult, the tone would have been almost pompous; coming from a youngster, it was closer to touching. 'I'm Jem McKay.' He hesitated. 'You send messages, don't you?' His voice cracked on the last word, and she heard his little hiss of aggravation at the slip.

'That's right, Jem. That's exactly what we do. I can call your parents and simply give them a message for you, or I can set up a meeting——'

'*No.* No meeting,' he broke in decisively. 'If you'd just send a message, please . . .'

'Okay,' Jolian agreed easily. There was no use pushing it. At least now he knew that a meeting could be arranged. And often a message was the start towards reconciliation anyway. 'What would you like me to say, Jem?' She picked up a pen and reached for her notepad.

'Er . . . there's just one thing, Jolian . . .' The boy stopped, obviously struggling with how to say it. 'You can't . . . you won't . . . tell him what part of the country you're calling from, will you, please?' The last few words tumbled out with a squeak and he hissed again.

'No,' she soothed. 'Not unless you want me to.'

'No!' It was almost a shout. He laughed shakily. 'He'd tear Boston apart brick by brick looking for me, if he knew where to look, Jolian. You can't tell him!'

Jolian grinned sympathetically. A formidable father, indeed. 'Ho-kay, mum's the word, Jem. I won't tell. Now, what's your message?'

'Tell him . . .' the boy paused again, then muttered quickly, 'Tell him "Happy Birthday".'

'Okay . . .' Now that wasn't too bad a start, Jolian thought hopefully. 'Anything else, Jem?'

'Umm, yes, please. You tell him if he hurts Ralph, I'll never speak to him again in my whole life!' Suddenly he was all small boy, desperate and angry.

Jolian hesitated, mentally starting the report she'd write on Jem for the file. Possible child abuse in family . . . 'Has he ever hurt Ralph before, Jem?' she asked gently.

'No, but Dad always said he'd sling him out the upstairs window if he ever jumped on his bed.' The boy sighed heavily. 'And that's just where Ralph'll want to sleep now that I'm gone.'

Jolian covered the mouthpiece and stifled her laughter against the back of her hand. She took a deep, careful breath. 'Okay—hands off Ralph if he ever wants a truce.' Her grin kept coming back, threatening to burst into a laugh again. 'Anything else, Jem?'

He thought a moment. 'No, I guess that's it, Jolian. Just don't let him trick you into saying where I am. He's tough.'

Jolian smiled again. 'He sounds it! So what's his phone number, Jem?' The boy recited it without hesitation, including the area code for Chicago. Jolian's brows lifted as she scribbled it down. He was a long way from home. 'In case I can't reach him here, Jem, do you know his number at work? I could try to get him tomorrow then.'

The boy laughed—a surprisingly bitter sound. 'That *is* his office number, Jolian. He's never home before nine or ten.'

'I see,' Jolian said carefully. 'Is there any other place I could reach him?'

The boy sighed again. 'No. He could be at Marisa's, or Barbara's or Jennifer's, or . . . No,' he said decisively, 'the best place is the office. He always comes back there.'

The office, or a girl-friend's place. Not home. Jolian was beginning to get the picture. 'Jem, what if he has a message for you? Would you want to hear it?'

'N-no,' the boy said quietly. 'Not really. It wouldn't be any use.' He was gathering his aloofness around him like a cloak. Any minute he would hang up now.

Jolian had a sudden inspiration. 'Does he know what to feed Ralph and how much?'

'Er . . . I . . . *think* so . . .' Adult resolve faded into small boy indecision.

'Maybe you should call me back, just in case he has any questions about that for you?' Jolian suggested helpfully. The job was to maintain contact, any sort of dialogue, keep them in touch no matter how tenuous the connection might be. At the same time, any way she could build up rapport between herself and the boy was all to the good.

She could feel him thinking, suspicion and independence balancing against the need to talk, to be connected to someone, even if it was just a friendly voice at the end of a phone line. Connection won out. 'Okay,' he answered finally. 'When do you work there?'

He was bright, all right, Jolian decided. Most kids somehow assumed that the first volunteer they spoke with *was* the hotline, a faceless friend on tap day and night. They were always a little crushed when they found their confidante was just one of many volunteers, available only a few hours each week—not a guardian angel, but an adult with a job and a family and a bed to crawl into most nights. 'I'll be here day after tomorrow, Jem, in the afternoon and early evening. Could you call me then?'

'Yes, Jolian. I'll make a note in my appointment book right now,' he said solemnly. 'Friday afternoon. I believe I can work that in.'

Jolian was amused. Yes, she supposed he did have a little extra time on his hands right now. It must be an odd, lost feeling not to be in school in September for the first time in his young life. She wondered suddenly if he was parodying his father as well as teasing her. 'Have you got a place to sleep, Jem?' she asked quickly.

But with that, she had stepped over some invisible line. 'I can take care of myself, Jolian.' The tone was decidedly distant.

'Well, good,' she said briskly. It was time to back off. 'I'll give your father your message and I'll be talking with you Friday, then—okay, Jem?'

'Okay.' His voice was suddenly gruff. 'And . . . thanks, Jolian.' The phone went dead.

Well. Jolian replaced the receiver thoughtfully. Interesting. That had not been the typical runaway call at all. Jem sounded quite a bit brighter, better educated than the usual waif. She shrugged. But if unusual, Jem was no freak, either. Alienation between parent and child was a classless epidemic in America. The children of the rich, as well as the poor, were running away. If only they would stop and wonder about what they were running towards . . . Her wide, slim shoulders hunched as she thought of Suzie, and then she shoved the thought aside. To survive on the hotline, you had to practise a certain humane detachment—a detachment that came hard to her quixotic nature. Failing detachment, at least a sense of humour was essential. *Pizza, my*—she grinned again.

Katy still murmured little listening sounds on the phone in the outer office. She had a talker there, apparently. Jolian glanced at her watch. Twenty minutes until David and Tracy Mullins came to relieve them. She pulled the phone towards her and began to dial.

'McKay Enterprises. May I help you?' The voice that answered on the first ring had the chilled-velvet tones of a first-rate receptionist.

'Yes. May I speak to Mr McKay, please?' So it was Jem's father's company. Somehow she was not surprised. Jolian captured a lock of hair and tickled her nose with it absently, rehearsing her message.

But it wasn't going to be that simple after all. 'I'll see if he's in right now. Who may I say is calling, please?' The cool voice left Jolian in no doubt that McKay was 'in' for some select individuals, and 'out' for others.

'Jolian Michaels. It's on urgent, personal business, please.'

But the elegant voice was not impressed. 'Thank you. Please hold.' The line went blank and Jolian swivelled her chair around to stare out of the grimy bay windows. To the west of the low buildings of Kenmore Square, the sky glowed luminous pink. The days were getting noticeably shorter already . . .

'Gillian, don't tell me you're broke again!' The male voice that spoke abruptly in her ear sounded half exasperated, half amused.

Jolian grinned. 'Wrong lady, Mr McKay. This is Jolian with a J and an o.'

There was a moment of thoughtful silence. 'Jolian as in Jo, who takes her Martinis without olives?' he tried finally. His voice was pleasantly low, and smooth as good whisky, with just a trace of bite to it.

Jolian laughed softly. This was absurd. But somehow it was amusing to twit the formidable Mr McKay. 'No, it's Jolian who takes her olives without Martinis, Mr McKay. You don't know me. It's about your son.'

She heard the hiss of an indrawn breath. 'Where is he?' he barked so suddenly that she jumped.

'I . . . can't tell you that, Mr McKay, but I do have a message for you . . .'

'Jolian!' There was an underlying tension to his voice now that hinted at some emotion under precarious control. 'Before you say anything you might regret . . .

you sound rather young. Do you know the penalty for kidnapping?'

'*Kid*napp——'

'Do you know that I'm prepared to spend as much money and time as it takes to catch you and your friends?' The low, smooth voice was a corrosive half-whisper now, dropping like acid into her ear. 'Do you know that when—not *if*, Jolian—but *when* I get my two hands on you, a life sentence in prison will be the least of your worries?'

Jolian swallowed hard and found that she was pressed back in her chair, huddling away from this harsh promise. How had she let the conversation take this turn? 'Wait a minute,' she tried firmly.

'No, *you* wait a minute, Jolian. I've been waiting all week!' he rasped back. 'If, on the other hand, you'll give up this ugly little plan and give me my son back—today—I'm prepared to pay you ten thousand dollars in unmarked bills and to forget the mistake ... That's assuming you haven't hurt him in any way, of course.'

Jolian sat upright and took a deep breath, thanking her lucky stars that she wasn't a kidnapper, not a kidnapper unlucky enough to be holding this man's son anyway.

'Well?' he bit out. 'Take it or——'

'*Mr* McKay,' she cut in determinedly, 'I'm prepared to pay ten thousand dollars in unmarked bills to get a word in edgewise in this conversation! Now take *that* or leave it!' She heard him hiss, sounding so much like his son that she had to smile.

There was a long moment of freezing silence. 'So go ahead,' he said bleakly.

'I am not—repeat, *not* a kidnapper, Mr McKay, truly, and I've never even seen your son. I'm a volunteer in a non-profit-making organisation that mediates between runaways and their parents by phone, and I have a message from Jem for you.' Jolian gulped air gratefully. There, she'd got it out.

'Runaways!' McKay breathed harshly. '*Jem?* Why would he . . .' He hissed impatiently again. 'What's the message?'

Jolian smiled sadly, picturing a hard-driving businessman groping to reassess his facts. No doubt he was better prepared to deal with a dozen kidnappers than one lost and lonely teenage son. 'The message is "Happy Birthday", Mr McKay,' she said gently.

'Happy . . .' His low voice trailed away, and then he sighed heavily. When he spoke at last, the voice was gruffer. 'Anything else, Jolian?'

'Yes, Mr McKay. Jem says that you're to be nice to Ralph, if you ever want to see him again.'

'Be nice to Ralph,' McKay mused wonderingly. 'What did he think I'd do—dropkick the son of a polecat over the neighbour's rooftop? And what did you say your organisation is called, Jolian?'

The change of subject left her flatfooted. 'Ah——' But a man who could command the resources to nab kidnappers could certainly trace the whereabouts of the Reachout office if she told him that, she decided quickly. 'I didn't.'

'Well, will you?'

'No, Mr McKay.'

'Well, who the hell's side are you on, you——' His voice ground suddenly to a halt, and as he took a deep breath, she dropped the answer neatly into the break.

'Jem's side.'

'Well, that's clear enough,' he snarled, 'I'm prepared to pay for that information, of course.'

'Of course you are,' Jolian told him sweetly, unable to resist the opening. 'But I'm not prepared to sell.' She heard the Mullins shuffle into the outer office. 'Now if you'll excuse me, Mr McKay . . .'

'Jolian, *wait!*' he demanded harshly, '. . . please . . .' The hiss following that plea told her what the word had cost him. 'Will you call me back?'

'Only if Jem has another message for you, sir.'

'Message,' he repeated softly. 'He *is* calling you back, then?'

'Yes. He promised to call me on Friday.'

'Friday? Jolian . . .' He stopped, and when he spoke again his voice had warmed to that tone he'd used in his first few words, 'Jolian . . . would you please call me, whether there's a message for me or not, after you talk with Jem on Friday?'

'Mr McKay, I can't use this line, except to send messages,' she told him gently. 'That's a rule. We have to watch our expenses.' Speaking of which, she glanced at her watch. They'd been talking for nearly fifteen minutes now.

'But . . . wait, I've got to know something. Ask Jem . . . ask him . . . what to feed his miserable tomcat, will you, Jolian? He hasn't eaten in three days now. Will you do that for me? Please?'

Jolian smiled, suddenly wondering what this man looked like. He had a nice voice. 'I'll ask him,' she promised. 'Goodbye, Mr McKay.' David was standing in the aisle between the files, one russet eyebrow raised teasingly, and she made a face at him.

'Just till Friday,' McKay reminded her softly.

'Till Friday,' she agreed, reaching across to break the connection with a finger. A most persuasive type when he wanted his way . . .

'Your latest admirer, Jolian?' David strolled into the office and set a medical textbook on the desk.

'Hardly!' Jolian gathered her assortment of needle files and packed them and the silver into her shoulder bag. 'More like an irate parent.' Pulling back her thick hair, she twisted it into a loose knot at the back of her neck. She clipped it in place with the forged silver barrette she had made years ago in her first jewellery class and stood up. 'Now do I look like a kidnapper to you, David?' she demanded indignantly.

Grinning, the gangly redhead inspected her from her long, brown legs to the top of her smooth dark head. He nodded solemnly. 'Wink those big blue peepers just once and you can kidnap anybody you want to, Jolian, provided he's male and out of diapers.'

Jolian smiled and looked down again quickly. This was touchy ground. David had never quite understood why she had broken off with him two years ago, why she wouldn't let their friendship grow into something more, as he had put it. Luckily Tracy had come along a few months after their break-up, and that question had become moot. 'I mean kidnapping for profit, not pleasure, goon!' she said lightly.

'Take a business course first,' he advised, slouching into the swivel chair and reaching for his book.

She laughed and turned away, slipping between the filing cabinets. Perhaps she'd been crazy to let David go. Friendship, kindness—most women would be happy to settle for that much. Who was she to wish for fireworks as well? *Quite probably a fool, that's who*, she told herself sardonically.

In the outer office, Tracy was underlining passages in another textbook and Katy was still trapped on the phone. She rolled her eyes in despair. Her date with the rugby hunk was in half an hour. 'Don't let him ply you with bean sprouts,' Jolian warned her softly. She collected her ten-speed bike and headed for the stairwell.

Stopping outside the Greek pizza parlour which occupied the first floor of their building, Jolian pulled a deep breath. The chill air tasted of fennel, red peppers and baking bread, and her mouth watered. 'Later,' she said firmly.

The long, soft September twilight was folding across the city. To the east, the downtown skyline loomed pale against the darkening sky. Tiny golden rectangles twinkled high up in the velvet blue, marking the windows of the late and the ambitious—people like Jem's father who placed work before family.

A light turned to green on the avenue before her and the traffic rumbled into motion. Jolian swung on to her bike. Around her, Kenmore Square was holding back the dark with its evening light show: green lights, red lights, headlights of speeding cars, street lights, and the brightly lit restaurants and shops combined to make a pulsing, electric daylight.

Within this bright bubble, people sauntered or jogged, window-shopped or paused to talk and laugh on the wide sidewalks. It was a young crowd, many of them students from Boston University or the art institute just down the street. Perhaps Jem himself was here, Jolian mused as she eased into the stream of traffic and pedalled away. With its bright lights and youthful, happy throngs, Kenmore Square might well attract a young stranger. Reaching Massachusetts Avenue, she turned left, heading for the Harvard Bridge and Cambridge beyond. But then Boston was a large, a very large city, filled with bright lights and young crowds. The boy could be anywhere. *And he can take care of himself*, she reminded herself firmly. Her wide mouth twisted in a rueful, sceptical grimace, then she put him out of her mind as she pedalled out on to the bridge.

The exact middle of the long, low Harvard Bridge was one of Jolian's favourite haunts. She was late tonight, and Yaffa would be yowling the house down, but she stopped for just a minute to lean against the iron railing. Around her, the Charles River stretched away, a wind-ruffled field of silver-blue, and she took a deep, satisfied breath. From here, the dark and rushing streets of the city were just a blur and a murmur. Tilting her head back, Jolian could see the full expanse of sky for the first time that day. The feeling of space and distance, of peace, was lovely. Lovely—and quite suddenly—lonely. The river wind raised goosebumps across her thighs and she shivered. It would be cold tonight. Autumn was coming—slowly, but it was coming.

Pushing off again, she hoped Jem would find a warm place to sleep tonight, and Suzie ... Jolian shivered again. *Good luck tonight, poor Suzie.* She would need it. Turning left off the bridge in front of the massive buildings of the Massachusetts Institute of Technology, Jolian followed the river footpath to the west, cycling slowly past the puffing joggers. No, the best thing she could wish for Suzie was a cold and lonely bed tonight. *Like mine*, the thought popped into her head. Oh, *shut up*, she told herself firmly. *It's your own choice, after all. It's not as if you've had no offers.* She began pedalling faster, her eyes wide in the deepening twilight.

It was dark by the time she cut away from the river, across the parkway and into a quiet street lined with tall trees and three-storey Victorian houses. Her neighbourhood was a peaceful backwater tucked between Harvard, M.I.T. and the Charles river—a refuge for young professionals and older grad students, bachelor professors and widows who had lived there all their lives. Coasting around a second corner, she turned into a short dead-end street and then up a driveway beside a dark, angular house with high-peaked roofs and jutting dormers.

As Jolian climbed the back stairs to the third floor, she heard the phone ringing and the anguished yowls of an abandoned Siamese. Yaffa flowed out through the unlocked door and wove around her legs with piteous cries as Jolian stumbled across the dark kitchen to pick up the receiver. 'Hello?' She pulled a deep, laughing breath and then swayed as Yaffa landed on her shoulder with a throaty moan.

'Hello?' It was a man's voice, puzzled and a bit stiff, very correct.

'George,' she identified him as she lifted the small cat off her shoulder and dropped it. 'How are you?'

'I'm fine. What on earth was that?'

'One small and starving cat. I just walked in the door.' Stretching the phone cord across the room, Jolian flipped on a light. The long room which was kitchen at one end and living room at the other leaped into view, giving a swift impression of pale woods and large plants.

'So I gathered,' he said dryly. 'I've been trying to reach you all day. Where were you?'

Yaffa bounded on to the large butcher block table that divided the two areas, then leaped off again as Jolian aimed a swat at her. 'Oh, out and about,' she said gaily, tiptoeing for a can of cat food on one of the shelves above the counter. One coffee together and one movie-with-dinner date hardly obliged her to report her daily schedule to George, as far as she was concerned. Yaffa darted around her feet with short urgent cries as she dished the food out. 'I'm feeding her, not killing her, no matter what it sounds like,' she assured him cheerfully.

'And may I feed you tonight?' George offered quickly. He sounded just a trifle unsure of himself, or perhaps irritated. Or perhaps one emotion followed the other.

Jolian hesitated, then tossed the can-opener into the sink. In the window above it, her face was reflected, her deep eyes shadowed by thick lashes. It was a delicately strong face, self-possessed as a cat's, and not unlike a cat's with its high cheekbones and pointed chin. Self-possessed ... Her instincts said no tonight. 'Oh, perhaps not, George ... I'm pretty tired tonight. And I've got a new design I want to finish and give my partner tomorrow ...' But then her instincts always seemed to say no, where men were concerned. And was it fair to judge someone after one and a half dates? It was not. That conclusion lent an apologetic softness to her excuse which he was quick to seize on.

'Well then, what about Saturday, Jolian? There's a new French restaurant I want to try. I hear it's excellent.' He paused expectantly.

There was really no reason not to, Jolian thought regretfully. 'That sounds lovely, George. What time?' He was really quite nice, and eminently presentable— young lawyer on the way up, attractive, intelligent, family money. Just a little ... stuffy.

'Let's say six-thirty.'

'All right, George. I'll see you then.' Talk of French restaurants had roused her stomach again. Jolian found a carton of raspberry yogurt in the fridge and ate it on her feet as she paced slowly around the living room with its low sofas and its tall potted palm trees edging the cream-coloured walls.' She stopped before the crammed-full bookcase along the inner wall to study the titles and then turned away again. Odd how restless and ... lonely ... she was tonight. Usually solitude didn't bother her at all.

'I thought you wanted to be alone?' she mocked herself. The branches of the elm outside stroked softly against the room-length bank of windows which faced the back yard and she shivered suddenly. 'Well, I don't,' she told the cat that padded on to the rug at her feet and sat to lick a dark paw. 'All I really want is someone to love ...' No more than that. And no less. *No less*, she repeated fiercely, scowling down at the carpet. Her eyes refocused on the cat and she smiled suddenly, shrugged and scooped Yaffa into her arms. Yaffa sniffed her chin and Jolian drew back, her nose wrinkling. 'Yuk! Let me rephrase that. All I want is someone to love, who doesn't smell like last year's tuna fish!' Cat in arms, she wandered into the jewellery shop she had set up in the front bedroom. Work would cure this. It always did ...

There was no time to be lonely, little time to think of lost children, still less to worry about anguished parents in the next day and a half of Jolian's life, She completed the piece, which would be a prototype for a new line of reversible bracelets, and took it over to her partner's loft in Charlestown. With a few modifications, Al liked it and they worked out the production details over lunch, debating colours of stone to be used, whether the bezels should be gold or silver like the rest of the bracelet, and size of the first production run. She stayed to inspect a shipment of rings of Al's that two apprentices were finishing for a gallery in Miami, came up with an idea for a new improved version of that design, and spent half the afternoon trying to convince Al that it would be economically feasible to produce. Leaving him finally with threats and promises to construct the prototype herself, Jolian barely made it back to Cambridge in time to teach her night course on beginning jewellery-making at the local high school. Her students—as eager and clumsy a bunch as she'd ever taught—broke an average of five sawblades apiece, and by the end of the evening, her face ached from trying not to laugh.

Friday started slower and sweeter. Too sweet, Jolian thought ruefully as she brushed in a wash of Payne's Gray on her rendering of a sterling silver pendant. Al would gag if he saw these saccharine concoctions of hearts and flowers she was creating for a custume jewellery house in Rhode Island. They were a far cry from the elegant, simple, and costly designs with which Quicksilver Designs was making its name. But then, money was money. Those first two years while Al and she had scrabbled for every penny to keep Quicksilver in soldier and silver were too vivid a memory; it was still hard to turn work down. Perhaps in another year or two, if Quicksilver continued its present comet ride, she could stop hustling, feel secure enough to pick and

choose her commissions . . . if she need do any outside
designing at all. 'In the meantime, I won't tell Al, if you
won't,' she promised Yaffa. Front paws tucked beneath
her, Yaffa sat under the desk lamp like a small broody
hen. She blinked blue eyes and said nothing.

Jolian consulted her watch. She was due for her shift
at the hotline in an hour and a half. She stood up and
stretched.

'So help me, Jolian, he didn't even put oil in the salad
dressing! Just herbs and lemon juice. And no butter
with the bread—I thought I'd starve!' Katy stopped to
take a gulp of coffee as if she were still starving. 'I
kissed him goodnight, shut the door, and just *bolted* for
the refrigerator!'

Jolian laughed and leaned back in her swivel chair,
stretching her long denim-clad legs out beneath the
desk. The afternoon had turned grey and misty and she
had dressed warmly for her bike ride to the office. Her
dark blue sweater echoed the colour of her laughing
eyes. 'So will you go out with him again, if he asks,
Katy, risking certain starvation in the quest for love?'

Katy looked guilty. 'As a matter of fact, Jolian, I
have a favour to ask——'

The phone on Jolian's desk rang. 'Don't tell me, I
can guess,' she groaned as she picked it up. 'Reachout
Hotline. Can I help you?'

'Jolian?'

'Jem,' she identified the boy warmly. 'How are you?'

'Oh, terrific. Just super! Peachy keen!' he blurted
bitterly, his voice cracking.

'I'm sorry.' She answered his tone, rather than the
words, and then they both laughed at how that
sounded. 'Well, you know what I mean! Can I do
anything?'

'You're doing it,' he answered awkwardly, sounding
very young and very gallant.

'Oh.' What a neat kid! *Come back in twenty years*, she thought quickly. 'Well, I did speak with your father, Jem.'

'How is he?' The question was nearly inaudible, and behind it, she heard a car start up. He must be at an outside phone booth.

'Worried. Upset . . . I think . . . surprised that you ran away.' Why *had* he run, anyway?

Jem laughed shortly. 'Of course he's surprised. What would he know?'

'He wants you back, Jem.' She tried to make that a neutral statement, not to coax, but perhaps the words were too soft.

'Sure he does,' the boy said coldly. 'He never starts a job unless he means to finish it and finish it right.' His breath hissed in her ear. 'What about Ralph? Is he okay?'

'It sounds like your father's doing his best with him,' she said carefully, 'but he's not eating much. Maybe he's missing you?'

'Probably.' The boy's voice was glum. 'Did he say what he's feeding him?'

Jolian picked up a pen and began to doodle on the pad before her. 'Well, as a matter of fact, Jem, he asked me to ask you what to give him.' Crouching by a dish heaped with food, a fat, sullen cat began to take shape.

'I wonder if he forgot to pour a little cream on his dry food?' the boy murmured. 'I thought he knew to do that . . . You didn't tell him where you were calling from, did you, Jolian?' His voice sharpened suddenly.

'No, Jem,' Jolian shook her head, 'I didn't. Honest.' She gave the cat a lashing tail and disgruntled whiskers. 'Do you want me to remind him about the cream, and see how Ralph's doing?'

There was quite a silence. Somewhere, at his end, a car honked. 'Would you?' he mumbled finally.

'Sure, Jem. Want me to tell him anything else?' She waited hopefully.

'Jolian?'

'Yes, Jem?'

'You're a sweetheart, Jolian, but it's no use.' He sounded closer to forty than fourteen, distantly amused by her transparency.

Jolian smiled wryly. He was a tough little son of a gun. 'Well, I'm sure Ralph will appreciate the effort,' she said lightly.

'So do I.'

It was time to test the connection then. Her chair squeaked as she leaned forward. 'Would you do me a favour, in that case, Jem?'

In the silence, she could feel him calculating the possibilities and perhaps his debt. 'Okay,' he said finally.

'Would you call me next week, Jem, Tuesday or Thursday afternoon, and just let me know how you're doing?'

For a long minute, she waited for him to hang up on her. When he spoke again his voice was brittle. 'I bet that's part of the training, isn't it, Jolian? How to answer the phone, how to sound like you really care about perfect strangers . . .'

'Jem?' she cut in softly.

'Um?'

'Don't be a sap.'

The sound that jerked out of him might have been a laugh. '*Okay*, Jolian . . . g'bye.'

Dial tone buzzing in her ear, she sat frowning at the far wall. 'Okay, I won't be a sap,' or 'okay, I'll call you?' 'You blew it, you chump!' she said aloud. She'd pushed too far, too fast. Still scowling, she hung up the phone. Blew it! She gave her chair an exasperated spin and glared at the miserable grey day as it rotated into view. What a rotten day to be young, alone, and unloved in the city. Rotten!

'You all right in there?' Katy called from her desk.

'Why shouldn't I be?' The chair was slowing down and the office glided by in all its green-painted dinginess.

'Well, your chair's going round.'

'Oh.' Jolian grabbed the edge of the desk and stopped herself. 'No, everything's just——' The phone rang out and Katy picked it up in the other room. 'Peachy keen,' Jolian muttered bitterly. She yanked open the shoulder bag on her desk and began to pull out tools and a small box. Might as well do something useful.

But she was too irritated to work. Jewellery-making called for patience, serenity, steady hands. No doubt that was why she preferred designing to construction. Jolian put the project down again and scowled at the cat doodle on the desk before her. So how was the son of a polecat, anyway? Her lips twitched and then curled upwards in a low, unwilling grin. She reached for the phone.

'McKay Enterprises. May I help you?' It was the receptionist with the air-conditioned voice again.

'Yes, please. This is Jolian Michaels. Mr McKay asked me to call him this afternoon.'

The elegant voice thawed perceptibly. 'Oh, *yes*, Ms Michaels, he mentioned you. Would you hold one moment, please?'

The moment turned into a minute, possibly two. Jolian picked up the ring of cast silver on her desk and squinted at it thoughtfully. It was a lost-wax casting, a process she'd not used much before. She was going to like it.

'Miss Michaels?' It was the receptionist again, warmly apologetic now. 'Mr McKay is on the line with another client. I gather it's a bit of an emergency. Would you mind waiting a minute or so?'

'Not at all.' The phone went dead again and Jolian was left to wonder just what *was* an emergency in the life of Mr McKay, if a missing son was not. She turned the ring in her hands. This was a private project, a Christmas present for her mother, but already it was giving her ideas . . . She picked up the pen and began to sketch.

'Miss Michaels?'

Jolian jumped as the receptionist came back on the line. 'Yes?' She glanced at her watch. Five minutes! The sketch before her was nearly complete, but this was getting to be a bit much.

'Thank you for your patience. Mr McKay will be just a few more minutes.'

'That's all right, I'll—call back,' she finished ruefully, but no one was listening. She was back on hold. Fuming, Jolian glanced at her watch. She'd give him just two more minutes. She studied her sketch and then looked back at her watch, waiting for the second hand to twitch round again. So what *was* important to this man?

'Miss Michaels?' The receptionists's soothing tone warned her. 'I'm really quite sorry, but Mr McKay's still on the other line. He asked me to take your message—it's instructions for feeding a cat, isn't it?'

So *that* was how much he cared! Jolian thought savagely. No wonder Jem couldn't believe she honestly cared about him! She gave the brief feeding instructions in icy, clipped tones and prepared to hang up.

'Jolian!' The whisky-smooth voice of Jem's father broke into her farewell. 'Miss Howard, we're nearly set and thank you *very* much,' he said buoyantly. There was a click as the receptionist hung up. 'Jolian, are you still there?'

Jolian picked up her pen and slashed a savage lightning bolt above the sulking cat. 'Just . . . barely,' she managed through her teeth. And a fat lot he cared, either!

But Mr McKay was making a long-winded and seemingly sincere apology, something about a factory burning down in Tennessee and the problem of getting quality products nowadays. Poor Jem. She sighed heavily.

'Jolian?' Mr McKay stopped in mid-sentence. 'Are you angry, by any chance?'

How could someone sound that warm and yet be so cold, so unfeeling? Jolian wondered bitterly. And was it her imagination, or was he possibly amused as well? 'Angry? Now why should I be angry, Mr McKay, just because the phone's grown to my ear?' she cooed. 'I just *love* waiting.'

'Then you know how I've felt these last two days, Jolian.' His voice had changed again. All the warmth was gone. 'With nothing to do but wait and wonder where my son is. Wonder if he's warm, safe, has anything to eat. Wonder if a certain righteous little do-gooder will even bother to call me back at all.'

Righteous do-gooder! 'Well, thanks!' she said bitterly. 'Your secretary has the feeding instructions for Ralph. There was no other message. Goodbye, Mr——'

'Jolian?' There was a warning note to his voice which stopped her cold. 'Jolian, this is the last time I'll ask you . . . nicely. Where is my son?'

Jolian sighed. 'Mr McKay, I can't tell you. Not even if I knew.'

'What city is he calling from? If I know that, I can notify the police, hire detectives, put out posters, offer rewards . . .' There was a passionate conviction to his words, the conviction of the hard-driving businessman that all problems will yield to the right combination of energy and money, even problems of the heart.

As if he could see her, Jolian shook her dark head. 'Mr McKay, I can't tell you.'

He took a deep breath and then let it out slowly. 'But you will, Jolian,' he promised softly. 'You will.' There came a gentle click, and then the dial tone buzzed in her ear.

And what did he mean by that? An odd little shiver skated across her shoulders and, slowly, Jolian put the receiver down. She swung the chair around to stare out the bay windows. What a cold, raw, menacing afternoon, 'You will.' It has been a threat, no less than a promise. She shivered again and then laughed at herself. 'First, Mr McKay, you have to find me,' she whispered defiantly.

CHAPTER TWO

Slow and damp as a slug, the afternoon crawled past. They took several calls. A girl with a dreadful cough called from Connecticut, wanting her mother in Maine to send her the bus fare home. The mother refused, and they referred the girl to a runaway shelter where she would find counselling and health care. A boy wanted his sister to know that he was all right and living with friends, not to worry. Katy answered the phone once, to hear nothing but sobs. Whoever it was tried to speak, couldn't, and hung up, still sobbing. A dreary afternoon.

Katy's favour turned out to be a plea that Jolian take the extra evening shift which Katy had signed up for a week ago. An emergency in the form of a certain rugby hunk had come up; she was invited to a movie tonight—and moaning loudly, Jolian agreed. Who was she to stand in the path of true love, after all? With any luck, she would finish the ring, and besides, no one waited for *her* tonight, if you didn't count a certain undersized, loud-mouthed cat. A depressing afternoon.

The lights came on early down in the square below, smudging the dark pavement with gleaming colours, and a grateful Katy nipped out to buy Jolian some egg rolls before deserting her. It was blatant bribery, but Jolian ate them anyway. Katy's replacement was an older woman whom Jolian didn't know, and she didn't talk much. They each worked at their own desks, the woman reading quietly, Jolian setting pearls into the ring with the tip of her tongue caught between her teeth.

Cars swished in the street below and somewhere a door slammed. Slow footsteps climbed the stairs.

31

'Jolian?'

She jumped nervously and cramped fingers lost their grip on the ring. It landed in her lap and the pearl she had been fitting bounded away. She swore softly. 'Yes, Ellen?'

She was standing in the aisle by the filing cabinets, purse in hand. 'I've got to run down the hall to the ladies' room, dear. I won't be too long.'

'No problem, Ellen.' Jolian looked down again quickly. The pearl didn't seem to be in her lap, but then she hadn't heard it fall. That meant it was probably in the remnant of shag rug under the desk rather than out on the age-splotched linoleum. Putting her feet down warily, she slid out of her chair and knelt behind the desk, her eyes combing the carpet.

'Excuse me, is this . . .' A male voice out in the hallway rumbled a question and Jolian heard Ellen's softer voice replying. But where had the beastly pearl got to? Stroking her fingers slowly through the worn shag, she crawled under the desk, wishing for a flashlight; it was dark under here.

The office door opened and the man's voice came clearer now, low and smooth. 'Yes, we're old friends.'

Crouched on hands and knees, Jolian paused and lifted her head, frowning. Where had she heard that voice before?

'Around to your left,' Ellen called helpfully. Her footsteps clicked away down the hall and faded out of hearing, leaving a soft, deep silence—a *listening* silence. A silence broken suddenly by the door's closing squeak. Jolian felt the hairs on the back of her neck stirring . . . No, it couldn't be . . .

Slow, deliberate footsteps crossed the linoleum as she froze, her fingers digging into the carpet. They paused by the filing cabinets and in the stillness she could hear her heart pounding. How could McKay have——

On came the footsteps. Bending her head down

slowly, she could see the light reflecting off dark leather with a soft gleam. Big feet.

They paused just inches from her face and she took a long, soft breath. He would be studying the desk now, staring down at her tools. Jolian heard his breath hiss—impatience, or—her eyes widened. Her chair, could it possibly still be rocking? Slowly, with infinite care, she turned her head to see.

Thank heavens, it wasn't—'*Oh!*' Bolting upright, she cracked her head on the desk above as a hand found her ankle.

'Jolian Michaels, I presume?' Laughter lurked just beneath the smooth surface of that low voice. Hard fingers squeezed her gently and let go.

Stars . . . She was really seeing stars . . . Jolian shook her head quickly, and the stars turned to comets.

'Will you be coming out, or shall I come in?' the low voice enquired politely.

He *was* laughing. And it wasn't stars she was seeing, Jolian decided, it was red. Teeth clenched, she crawled out and turned, still kneeling, to face him with frigid, dizzy deliberation.

He was tall. She had to tilt her head back to meet those dark eyes. One black eyebrow rose lazily and she saw the corner of his mouth twitch. 'I haven't played hide and seek in years,' he said gravely.

It was hard to get the words out, her teeth were clamped so tight. 'I lost something,' she gritted at last.

The other corner of his mouth tilted up to make a faint smile. 'Your nerve?' he suggested helpfully, taking a step forward.

Under his foot, a tiny, distinct crunch sounded, and Jolian's eyes widened. Not trusting herself to speak yet, she rose carefully and slid backwards into her chair. Stretching cramped legs out before her, she leaned back to gaze up at him, her fingers laced precisely over her flat stomach, her thick hair fanning out across her shoulders. 'No, Mr McKay,' she drawled pleasantly, 'I lost a pearl. The one you're standing on.'

And it was worth every penny to see his dismay. For one moment the macho façade slipped as he balanced on one foot, scowling at the sole of his shoe, his brows drawn together in a dark line. For that second, Jolian had a glimpse of a gawky boy not yet grown into his treacherous feet. When he looked up again, it was gone. A man faced her, incredibly attractive, icily controlled, quite determined to regain control of this interview. Reaching into his coat pocket, he pulled out a wallet. 'How much, Jolian?'

Her mocking smile widened. Priceless. Money solves everything, doesn't it? 'No charge, Mr McKay. You came a long way to step on that pearl. It was my pleasure.'

'How *much*?' he repeated, his brows drawing together dangerously.

Slowly, still smiling, she shook her head again. She had his goat already; that was payment enough.

But the care with which he removed the bill from his wallet was an indication of rage, not irritation, she realised belatedly. And there was no place to retreat as he advanced upon her; she was leaning as far back in her chair as she could, already. Defiantly, she stared up at him, determined to call this bluff . . . if bluff it was.

But something in her upturned face made him smile. 'Ever eaten a hundred dollars before, Jolian?' he asked gently. A large hand brought the folded bill up to her chin and he drew it in a slow, tickling caress along her jaw.

He would *not* scare her. He *would* not. Defiantly she held his gaze, then found herself held. She couldn't break away from those dark eyes. They weren't brown after all, but hazel—a dark green flecked with gold, deep and sardonic. She licked dry lips. 'Is it unmarked?' she asked shakily, speaking the words against the bill as he brushed it slowly across her lips. This wasn't really happening, was it?

His smile slowly deepened. 'Doubt it,' he whispered.

The edge of the bill traced the underside of her full bottom lip and his thumb dragged slowly after it, warm, subtly menacing. The pulse in her throat was hammering, making it hard to breathe, harder to swallow. 'Stop it!' she whispered, her eyes widening.

But the tip of the bill teased the curving line between her lips. Reaching up, she caught his wrist. It was hard and quite large, warm, the pulse racing. It carried her hand along as he feathered the bill across her throat. '*Stop* it!'

Green, gold, the eyes above her were coming closer. His smile would be wider now, she guessed, but she couldn't look down to make sure. Green, gold, too close—she shut her eyes to shut him out, but he found her anyway, took her lips in the dark . . .

So hot . . . So gentle . . . So slow . . . It wasn't what she'd expected at all. She had braced herself to meet a brutal kiss, a physical display of male supremacy, but he was more subtle than that. The warm lips which traced her mouth weren't taking her kiss so much as finding it, finding it with a touch so sure and gentle that she responded without thought. Her lips parted and the kiss deepened slowly, inevitably . . . irresistibly. There were many ways to dominate, weren't there?

Beneath her, Jolian felt as if the chair were falling slowly, ever so slowly, backwards. In the dark, her grip tightened on his wrist, but still she was falling, pulling him with her in a slow-motion, free-falling backdive. Only the feel of those wandering, questioning, moving lips was real. And this was insane!

Her eyes flashed open as those lips freed her at last, and he was smiling. Naturally. Pushing off against his wrist, she slewed the chair around and glared out of the window. But the window was all reflection: wide-eyed, duped and dizzy girl in front of dark business suit enclosing lean, muscular, overwhelmingly male body.

She refused to look higher, to meet those eyes that would be gleaming down at her now in masculine triumph.

The reflection stirred, an arm lifted, and something fluttered down on to her knees. 'And worth every penny,' he said huskily.

From her lap, Benjamin Franklin stared up at her. Another self-satisfied, overbearing, masculine ... *pig!* She crunched his face and launched him over her shoulder.

But McKay plucked her missile out of the air at chin height. It figured. Bitterly, she met his dark gaze in the reflection and found he wasn't smiling after all. Somehow that was even more disturbing. She looked down again quickly as he turned away.

And how was she to feel? Outrage chased confusion and something else in a dizzying swirl around her brain and came up headache as she watched him prowl the office behind her. She'd bumped her head, hadn't she? Perhaps everything that followed that was delirium. Any minute now, the arrogant, restless shape making coffee at the back counter would simply—coffee?

'Coffee?' Behind her, McKay's reflection set a mug on her desk, then stood back to sip from another. Dark eyes, narrowed in thought, watched her from over the rim as he drank.

Figments don't serve you coffee, Jolian concluded reluctantly. McKay would not simply vanish, he would have to be dealt with. Slowly she wheeled around to face him.

He saluted her return to the world with a flick of his half-smile and then watched in silence as she drank. Unnerving. Behind a hedge of eyelashes, Jolian concentrated on the bitter drink, ignoring the loom of him. After a moment, he sat on the edge of her desk, but still he towered above her; he was just closer now. Too close. Finally, his empty mug clicked on the desk beside her hand. 'So let's talk about Jem, now.'

She looked up to find those dark eyes waiting. 'I've told you all I have to tell, Mr McKay. You've wasted a trip, coming here.'

But slowly he shook his head. 'I don't think so.' His eyes roamed over her face and the smile flicked again. 'He's here in Boston, isn't he?'

Jolian looked down at the sketch pad before her. She reached out and picked up her pen, tapped it point down across the paper. 'We have a toll-free number here, Mr McKay. We take calls from all over the country.'

'Yes, I know that now.' Above her, a smile deepened the low voice. 'But Jem's here all the same, isn't he?'

She looked up at him, and then wished she hadn't, as his eyes caught and held her gaze. 'I didn't say that.'

His half-smile became a whole. 'What's the matter, Jolian, can't you lie? All you have to say is "No, Fletch, he isn't here".'

Fletch. An odd name. It was an effort to wrench her eyes away and down. She found the pad before her covered with big, wobbly stars. Automatically, she drew a careful five-point star, then a six-pointer.

A knuckle hooked under her chin and tilted her head back to meet that searching green gaze. 'I didn't know there were any Puritans left in Boston,' he murmured, one brow lifting slowly. 'Can't lie, takes her kissing seriously——'

Jolian jerked her chin away and looked down again. She chose the largest star and began constructing rainbow lines between its points. The office door creaked open and she heard Ellen clicking discreetly across the floor towards her desk. Some help she had been! Should she call her?

Standing, she met McKay's brow-raised, mocking gaze. No, it was too late to run yelling for help. This was her tiger. She gathered their mugs, took them back to the counter, and stopped short. In the collection

bowl, from among the dimes and quarters, a crumpled
Ben Franklin regarded her stonily. A hundred dollars.
The going rate for a pearl, a kiss, or two cups of lousy,
warmed-over coffee, the arrogant—wheeling, she found
him watching her. 'Why don't you just *buy* a new son,
Mr McKay, since money's no object?'

That brought his head up and his eyebrows down. 'If
I were buying flesh this minute, I'd not be after a son,
believe me, love. What's *your* price, by the way?'

Insufferable! Eyes flashing, she whipped her hair
back from a neck grown suddenly hot. 'It's out of your
range, and it doesn't come in a wallet!'

'No legal tender, hmm?' His dark eyes travelled
slowly across her body, heating it as they searched for
the price tag. 'So what kind of ... tender do you
accept?' Beside him, the phone rang and he reached for
it mechanically.

'Don't you touch that!' Jolian was across the room
before she realised it, her hand landing on top of his
fingers. He turned and their noses nearly touched. At
this range his eyes were enormous, deep pools of green
flecked with sunlight. The phone rang again, and in
spite of her downward pressure, he lifted the receiver.
His lips twitched at the look on her face and he held the
phone to her ear with mocking gallantry.

'Reachout Hotline,' she spoke automatically, beaming
her rage into his eyes. Any minute now he should burst
into flames.

'Jolian?' The girl's voice was a panting, throat-
straining whisper. 'Is that you?'

'Yes! Suzie? Are you all right?' Jolian squeezed the
receiver and stared through the clear eyes before her,
picturing instead a girl huddled over a phone in the
dark somewhere.

'No!' The girl swallowed audibly. 'I'm ... in trouble,
Jolian, I ...' Her voice caught in a whimper. 'It's Tony.
He wants me to ... to ... to ... to ...'

'To be a prostitute?'

'How . . .' the girl gulped and tried again, 'how did you know?'

Jolian fought back the angry laugh, kept her voice briskly confident. 'I'll tell you later, Suzie. Now tell me where you are. Are you out on the street?'

'Yes.'

'Do you know the name of it?'

'No,' the thread of hysteria tightened in her voice. 'No, he wouldn't——'

'What do you see, Suzie? Tell me.'

'Tall buildings, dirty bookstores, an X-rated theatre, ugly men—oh, *Jolian*——'

'Give me a name, Suzie,' she commanded quickly. 'What's right across the street from you?' And where was her pimp? He wouldn't be far away.

'The Pussycat Lounge——' Suzie was answering mechanically now, like a good child, but she was still panting.

'Okay, I know where you are, Suzie.' The Combat Zone, of course. 'I'll have the police there in five minutes.'

'*Police?*' The word shrilled wildly through the room. '*No! Jolian*, you c-c-c-*can't*——' Her voice fractured into a series of stuttering hiccups. 'My *mother* w-would . . .' Any second she would hang up now.

'All right, Suzie, no police. I won't call the police. Suzie, *listen* to me!' It was hard to shout and sound calm at the same time. 'Suzie, are you listening?'

The hiccup might have meant yes.

'I'll be there in ten minutes. I'll stop the car in front of the Pussycat Lounge. I'll honk the horn three times—beep, beep, beep. When I do, you come *running*, okay?'

'O . . . kay . . .'

'Right, now get off the phone before Tony sees you. Stand where he told you. If anyone asks you to go with him, say you're sick—very sick. I'll be there as quick as I can. Be brave, Suzie, and *listen* for me.'

Starting to hang up, Jolian discovered she still trapped McKay's fingers against the phone. Her other hand gripped his wrist in a stranglehold. He grinned as she blinked. 'Any time, General.' He replaced the receiver for her and stood up.

He was forgotten already. Bike—collect it later. Shoulder bag. She opened it wide, swept her tools into it and wheeled towards the door. 'Ellen, I need your car,' she announced, striding into the main office.

'No, she doesn't,' McKay told the open-mouthed woman as his hand closed on Jolian's arm. 'She's got mine. You hold the fort.' He opened the door and swept her out before him. 'Let's go.'

McKay's car was a four-door rental, double-parked in front of the pizza parlour. He pocketed a parking ticket without reading it, had them moving before she could slam the door. 'Where to?'

'Straight ahead, but stay right. We'll go right in about a mile.' She stared ahead eagerly, caught herself against the dash as the car slid between two taxis and accelerated away from a blare of horns and yells.

'Hang on,' he told her needlessly.

'Right. And right next corner.' Hooking an elbow over the seat back, Jolian turned to watch him. Looming headlights backlit the hard, straight lines of his profile for an instant, showed her his lips tucked up in that unrevealing almost-smile. The long-fingered hands on the wheel were relaxed. The dark eyes moved constantly, sparking as the street lights flickered past. He was enjoying himself, wasn't he? 'Okay, take a left here, Mr McKay.'

'Fletch,' he reminded her, cutting in front of a wall of oncoming traffic. His smile deepened as she gasped, then it faded again.

Jolian let out her breath slowly. 'An ... odd name.

I've never heard it before.'

Eyes on a fast approaching traffic light, he answered her absently. 'Family name—Fletcher. As in Fletcher Christian.' The light turned yellow and the car surged ahead. *'Mutiny on the Bounty?'*

'Oh.' His face flashed bloody as they swept under the light. Yes, he looked like a mutineer all right, or rather, a pirate, with that glinting, reckless look. Like a man with nothing to lose. Arrogant and outrageous as he was, she was suddenly glad he was here to help her . . . presuming they arrived alive.

He flicked a glance her way. 'Much further?' They were gliding through the dirty canyons that were the backside of downtown Boston now. The streets were darker here and the people moved differently. Some scurried with quick glances over tight shoulders. Others shambled blindly with heads down.

'No, just a few blocks. See the neon signs and the traffic up ahead? We turn left there.'

'Can you drive, Jolian?' McKay spared her another glance.

'Yes, why——'

But the car pulled over and stopped and he was out of his seat already, opening the back door. 'Scoot over and drive, then.' Kneeling on the floor behind the driver's seat he peered over her shoulder. 'Come on.'

Shakily, Jolian swung the car back into the traffic. It was getting thicker now, slow cruising, the passenger's heads craning as they scanned the crowded sidewalks and the store-fronts beyond. 'Why?'

His breath warmed her ear. 'She's expecting you, not a man. We don't want to scare her away. She sounded half out of her wits already.'

'Yes.' Jolian scanned the sidewalks ahead. Pictures of women on every grimy store-front, but few women on the street. One older woman walked slowly, hips swaying in her tight, cheap dress. Another lounged in a

doorway, eyes distant and dreaming. College boys in a
nervous, laughing huddle before a store offering
'ADULT books, rubber and leather goods.' 'LIVE
NUDES', promised one sign in neon red; 'BOSTON
BUNNIES', blinked another in flashing white light-
bulbs. Young men swaggered in blue jeans and
undershirts, a white-bearded man, staggered through
the trash in the gutter, a plumply dapper man in a
checkered suit dithered before a door offering
'PRIVATE BOOTHS—25¢.'

'Do you see her?' Fletcher McKay's voice came from
behind the seat now.

'I don't even know what she looks like!' Above a
dark entrance just ahead, a lighted marquee barely had
room among the rows and rows of X's to show the film
title in smaller print. And beyond that, a blue neon sign
flashed. A cat-eared woman with impossibly long legs
high-kicked the can-can ... kick ... off; down ... off;
kick ... off ... 'But there's the Pussycat!'

'Jolian, she's probably been picked up by now. But if
she comes, lock the door after her *immediately* and take
off, understand?'

'Yes.' Jolian swallowed and slowly, deliberately, hit
the horn. Once. Twice. Three times.

Faces in the car just ahead glared back at her,
mouthing soundless words; hands gestured obscenely.
But on the sidewalks, no one turned to look. The men
drifted on their way, absorbed in their endless prowl for
something money would never buy.

'Hit it again.'

Jolian rolled down her window, leaned out to show
herself and tapped the horn again. 'Suzie, where *are* you?'

Up ahead and across the street, a girl plunged
between two parked cars. Dressed in hot pants,
teetering on backless spike heels, eyes wild and mouth
open, she dodged blindly through the slow-moving
traffic. 'There she is!' Waving frantically, Jolian leaned

out of the window. *'Suzie!'* The girl staggered forward and caught herself against the car's hood, fingers spread wide, panting, staring through the windshield like a deer frozen in the oncoming headlights.

Jolian leaned over to throw open the passenger door. 'Suzie, get in!'

The girl blinked and moved again, leaning against the car as she hobbled around the front of it to half-fall inside. 'Jolian?'

'Yes, Suzie. Get your feet in and shut the door.' The girl scrabbled at it. From her movements and the smell of her, she was half drunk. Jolian leaned across her to help.

'Hey!' The door handle ripped out of her grasp just as Suzie shrieked in her ear. A snarling face and wide shoulders filled the doorway, thrust into the car. 'Whad'ya think yer doin'! Tha's *my* woman!'

His eighty-proof breath searing her face, Jolian reeled backwards to clutch at the steering wheel as the girl shrilled again. 'Tony, *no*!'

But one fist buried in the girl's long hair, he dragged her towards the door, his other hand groping in the pocket of his jacket. And he was smiling. 'I told ya, baby—cross me once an ya'd be sorry. Real sorry.' Crazed eyes on the squealing girl, he didn't see the man looming up behind the seat until large hands caught his wrists. *'Hey!'*

'Coming with us, punk?' Fletcher McKay's voice was low and deadly, the one sound of sanity in this shrieking bedlam. 'Drive, Jolian,' he commanded, grunting as the man struggled in his hold.

The pimp's feet were still on the ground outside; did McKay mean to——

'Drive!' he gritted. The pimp heaved beneath him, still fighting to get his right fist from his pocket. 'Come *on*, Tony, the cops'll . . . love you.'

Jolian stepped on the gas and moved out slowly.

'*Hey!*' Rage turned to alarm in the coarse voice as he stumbled alongside the car. 'Le' go!'

'Faster, Jolian. You sure, Tony? We've got lots of room here.'

'Lemme *go*!'

'Right you are ... *punk*.' McKay's tug turned to shove and Jolian saw the pimp sprawl backwards toward the kerb and sit down—hard. 'Step on it, Jolian.' McKay reached out to slam and lock the door, turned to stare back at his victim.

Jolian obeyed automatically, one hand on the back of the girl beside her. Huddled into near-foetal position, face hidden against her knees, Suzie was silent now, only her shuddering suggesting that she was still conscious.

And she was shivering too, Jolian realised as they turned a corner and picked up speed. God, if Fletcher McKay hadn't been there ...

'Pull over,' he directed suddenly. 'I'll drive.'

Obeying gratefully, Jolian wobbled around to sit outside the collapsed girl, sat stroking her tangled hair with shaking fingers as the car glided and turned through the dark streets.

Finally he spoke again. 'Okay, Jolian, no one's following us. What now?'

She looked up from the girl beside her. It took a moment to place herself. 'Oh ... okay. Go left at the next lights. We're taking the Mass pike out to Newton.'

Fletcher McKay swung the car into the turn. 'What's out there?'

Jolian stroked the girl's hair and spoke the words to her, making them almost a lullaby, a chant to call her back from the nightmare world in which she'd been lost. 'Oh ... a warm bath, something hot to eat, a bed with clean sheets ... and a good ... long ... sleep, for starters.' And tomorrow, some decisions to make with the help of Hannah Bernstein, child psychologist, and the hotline's crisis intervention expert. Underneath her hand, Suzie stirred and heaved a deep, slow sigh.

'That sounds like the ticket.' Above her, his low voice was warm and smiling.

It was nearly midnight when Jolian finally left Hannah's house in Newton and wandered back to the car parked out front. She felt as if she were floating. Was that the weight of Suzie lifting from her shoulders or just fatigue?

The damp night had grown no colder and Fletcher McKay had rolled down the car windows. He'd had quite a wait. Suzie had clung to her as the one known object in a world filled with uncertainty and menace. It had taken Hannah more than an hour to weave her motherly spell of comfort and common sense. At last the girl had dropped off from sheer exhaustion while they sat beside her bed, a night light glowing in the corner of the small pink bedroom, and Jolian had tiptoed away. Hannah, she suspected, would sit there all night.

Someone else had dropped off as well, she observed, leaning in at the window. Fletcher McKay had turned sideways to stretch his long legs out on the seat. His head was thrown back against the door at an awkward angle, but he slept with his mouth closed, she noticed approvingly. And a very nice mouth it was, too. Beautiful wasn't quite the right word for it, not masculine enough to describe its chiselled, perfectly defined form. And handsome was too trite . . .

One corner of that mouth lifted slowly in the dim light, and then the second. 'Think you'll be able to give the cops a complete description?'

It was too dark for him to see her blush, Jolian told herself firmly, getting into the car as he moved his legs. 'Sure. Tall, dark, and badly in need of a shave.' She grinned as his hand jerked towards his chin and then stopped.

He laughed under his breath. 'Badly in need of some food as well! Where can we eat, this time of night?'

Jolian frowned. In spite of his piratical jaw and tousled hair, and the split at the shoulder seam of his coat she spotted as they passed under a street light, Fletcher McKay did not look like a man who ate at greasy spoons and hamburger joints. She could think of nothing else that would still be open. At the very least, she owed him a decent meal. 'Take a right here, Mr McKay.'

'Try Fletch and I might.'

'Fletch,' she murmured reluctantly, and the car turned.

When at last they turned on to her street, nothing stirred, nothing but a few dry leaves scuttering before the damp breeze. He parked the car and looked around slowly. 'There's a restaurant here?'

'Best in town.' Suddenly this didn't seem like such a good idea after all. He wouldn't misinterpret this gesture, would he?

He followed her, tiptoeing obediently, up the two flights of stairs, one eyebrow raised slightly, an odd smile on his dark face. Suddenly he stopped, staring into the dark above. 'What in God's name was that?'

The sound came again, the anguished moan of a banshee with strep throat. 'That's what I'm cooking for your supper, if she wakes the neighbours!' Jolian bounded ahead of him, hissing threats at the cat as she unlocked the door. Yaffa poured out on to the landing, voicing feline complaints of starvation and woe, and scooping her up. Jolian turned to face her guest, jiggling the Siamese in her arms. 'Yaffa, meet Mr Fletcher McKay.'

Two steps below her, Fletch stopped, his dark brows drawing together. '*Cats*,' he said finally between his teeth. 'Marvellous animals.'

'That's all right.' Jolian transferred Yaffa to her shoulder and led the way into the room. 'She hates men, too. Just don't try to pet her.'

'No problem!'

He prowled the living room rather like a big cat himself while she fed Yaffa, put a frozen steak in the broiler and poured them each a glass of burgundy. The carpet muffled her footsteps as she came up behind him where he stood at the window. Close up, he was even taller than she'd thought; her head came up to his wide shoulders, no higher. 'Fletch?' He stiffened and then turned slowly, his dark eyes searching her face as she handed him his glass. 'Thank you for tonight,' she said softly. It was hard to speak when he looked like that. Words took on unexpected meanings, seemed to echo and evolve as they spun in the air.

He seemed to be listening to the echoes as well, as he took a slow, considering sip of the wine, his eyes never leaving her face. 'My pleasure.' He reached out to draw his glass slowly along her jawline, smiled slowly as her chin lifted away and she frowned. 'I couldn't let you run off to tilt with windmills all alone, you little lunatic. Do you do that often?'

She shook her head. No, tonight's rescue mission had gone far beyond the usual limits of hotline duty, emotional or physical. But there'd been no way to deny such a direct and personal call for help. If only Jane could have called five years ago ... She found his eyes still on her face and turned away from that measuring gaze to stare out of the window, listening to the elm leaves whisper in the dark. 'It's going to rain.'

His arm brushed her shoulder as he came to stand beside her, staring out into the night. 'Yes.'

And he was thinking of his son, she realised suddenly. 'He'll find someplace dry, Fletch. He said he could take care of himself.'

Beside her, he snorted, took another drink. 'That's what all fourteen-year-olds think, God help 'em. You saw how well they handle the real world tonight.'

Fourteen years. He must have married early—quite early. 'Why did Jem run?'

Wide shoulders lifted slightly as he took a long, deep breath. 'Damned if I really know, Jolian. I was hoping he might have told you. I haven't talked with Jem since July.'

'July?' Suddenly Jolian remembered the steak. She retreated towards the kitchen, staring back over her shoulder. 'July?'

He followed her and poured himself more wine, topped off her glass as well. 'It was one hectic summer, Jolian. I'm in the middle of a major deal—I've been putting that together since June. The housekeeper we've had since I—since Jem was six—moved to Texas. And Jem was running with a group of boys I didn't know and wasn't sure I liked. For all those reasons, it seemed a good time to pack him off to summer camp.' He leaned against the counter beside her, watching as she peeled an avocado for the salad.

'And when he came back from there?'

He sighed slowly. 'I was in California, Jolian, on this acquisition business. I'd intended to be home to welcome him, but I was delayed.' He drank again quickly and stared down at her hands, one corner of his mouth barely lifting in a rather hard half-smile. 'And then I stayed on a few more days,' he admitted wryly. 'I'd met an old . . . friend.' In spite of the toughness of that faint smile, or perhaps because of it, his words had the sound of a confession. They carried a load of quiet regret.

Jolian reached past him to rinse her hands at the sink. He didn't step back as she had expected him to and her shoulder rubbed across his hard chest. She flicked a glance up at him, frowning as his half-smile slowly became whole. No doubt about it, this man would have many . . . friends. Droves of them. Hordes. All he wanted and then some. She retreated to the cabinet and found half a loaf of French bread, stood staring at it for a moment. What next? It was hard to think with him so near ... Oh, set the table, of course. 'So what happened then?'

Scowling now, Fletch shrugged out of his coat and padded across to sling it over the back of a chair. 'He took some money I'd left around the house, just enough for a plane ticket to New York. Left me a polite little IOU, reminding me that I could repay myself from his savings account—he can't get at that without my co-signature. He convinced the new housekeeper—who's since been dismissed—that his mother had sent for him, and he flew off to New York to find her.' Head bent, he stared down at his wine glass, turning it slowly, the black brows a jagged line above the dark, thick lashes.

'And did he?' Jolian cut the steak, forked it on to two plates, brought them to the table, and sat.

'Hmm? Oh, yes.' He set his glass on the table and, still standing, loosened his tie, his dark eyes cold and distant. 'Liz entertained him for two weeks while—she claims—he dropped hints that she let him live with her. At the end of two weeks, she gave him his plane fare back to Chicago, patted him on the head, and showed him where the airport limousine stopped.' He whipped the tie off with a sudden vicious yank, stood holding it in his hand as if he'd never seen one before. 'That's the last anyone had heard of him, till he called you.' His angry, deep eyes lifted to her troubled face. He smiled crookedly and sat down.

'So she didn't want him,' Jolian mused as she buttered a slice of bread.

'She never wanted either of us.' It was a quiet, factual statement, stripped bare of all emotion, and it left her nothing to say. They ate in silence while she tried to picture a woman who wouldn't want this man.

They cleared the table together without speaking, and she turned down an offer to do the dishes. 'I'll do them tomorrow. No, I mean today ... Later.' She smiled sleepily and leaned back against the counter, blinking up at him as he checked his watch.

'Lord, Jolian, it's nearly three o'clock! Where's the nearest hotel?'

I shouldn't do this, she thought as she pointed at the convertible sofa under the windows. 'Right there if you want it, Fletch. It's a bit late to go hotel-hunting.'

The green-gold eyes stroked across her face in thoughtful appraisal. No doubt he was weighing how little or much this offer might mean. 'And where does your man-eating cat sleep?' he asked finally, half smiling.

Jolian muffled a yawn. 'She won't trouble you, Fletch. She sleeps with me.'

His half-smile completed itself slowly. 'Now *that* could trouble me plenty!' The smile deepened as her chin lifted dangerously, and he reached out to lay a fingertip across her parting lips. 'But not ... tonight.' As it dropped away, his finger pressed down gently, rolling her bottom lip out to graze the moist, soft skin just inside it. Another stolen kiss. Turning away before she could find her breath, he headed for the door. 'I'll get my bag, then.'

Not tonight! Jolian yanked out the sofa with savage, swift hands. The conceit of the man! As if all that kept them apart were his sleepiness and her cat! Not *tonight*. As if her willingness, no, her eagerness to jump into bed with him on any night at all was a foregone conclusion!

Selecting linens from the hall closet, she dumped them on to the opened couch and stalked back down the hallway towards the bathroom and her bedroom beyond. So let him make his own bed. She'd lost enough sleep over Fletcher McKay already.

It was some time later when Yaffa stirred and sat up in the circle of her arm. Jolian groaned and opened her eyes as the cat padded across her stomach and dropped to the bedroom floor. What now? She blinked up at the

ceiling, couldn't find it in the darkness above, a
murmurous, rushing darkness. Rain, that was it. Even
as she identified the sound, it seemed to gather and
swell. Downpour. Good night to be in bed. She
stretched luxuriously beneath the warm sheets and
rolled over, smiling, and remembered the open windows
in the living room. And Fletch. Damn. Would he wake
up? Have the sense to shut them? The rain always
seemed to blow in on that side of the house. She turned
over slowly to stare up towards the ceiling again. *Stop,
rain.* It was chuckling in the gutters now, thundering on
the low roof above her bed, mocking her command.
Surely he would wake up. Surely. *And if he doesn't, you
get to bail the living room in the morning*, she told
herself, sitting up reluctantly. *If you want something
done* . . . Slithering into the blue silk robe she'd bought
last month for two rings and a bracelet, she slipped out
the bedroom door, nearly closing it on Yaffa's probing
whiskers. She had to feel her way into the living room,
her eyes wide in the darkness. To her right, the sofa was
a dim, rumpled mass. The rattle of rain through the dry
leaves outside told her that the windows were indeed
still open wide. Before her, something stirred and she
stopped, picking out the tall shape at the window.
Fletch. Staring out into the night and the rain.

His head turned swiftly as she came up beside him,
then turned back again. 'It's not raining in yet?' she
asked softly.

'No, but it's sure as hell raining out.' His head leaned
slowly forward till it touched the screen. 'He's out there,
Jolian, somewhere. He catches colds at the drop of a
hat . . .'

'Fletch, stop!' She reached out to touch his arm and
then thought better of it.

'What the hell good's a father, if he can't keep a roof
over his own son?' He cursed softly, his forehead
brushing against the screen.

'Fletch, he's a bright kid. At the very least, he's under a bridge, in a phone booth, at the bus station . . .'

'That's quite a comfort, sweetheart. My kid among the winos, the bums, and the perverts. Thanks!'

Jolian turned to lean back against the windowsill, looking up at him, and realised suddenly that his muscular silhouette was too clean. He was bare-chested, and she didn't dare look lower. She swallowed. 'Look, Fletch, you're tired and there's nothing you can do about it tonight. Try to stop thinking about him.'

His breath hissed in a soft laugh, then he leaned towards her. She felt more than saw an arm go past her waist, found that she was trapped now between his arms and the windowsill. 'All right. But do you know what happens the second I stop thinking about Jem?'

Her voice would sound funny if she tried to speak now. She shook her head slowly and leaned backwards till her hair touched the screen. Trapped.

'I start thinking of doing *this*.' Warm fingers curled round her wrists, slid slowly upwards over the cool, slippery fabric that draped her arms.

'And *this*.' His hands followed the rounded, slim shapes of her upper arms up to her shoulders, glided up across those hollow, delicate planes to close lightly around her throat. The warmth of his hands on her bare skin was as shocking as the gesture. Jolian closed her eyes and pulled a deep, shivery breath. But the hands stroked on, caressing slowly up her neck till his outspread fingers combed into the thick, silky hair at the back of her head.

'Fletch . . .' Cupped in his arms, Jolian found her voice at last, or a shred of it anyway. The thrumming of the rain at her back was a sensation as well as a sound now, seemed to be inside the room as if warm, crystal raindrops shimmered across her bare skin. Raindrops falling in a tingling, throbbing dance across wakening flesh. 'Fletch, don't!'

'Don't what, my silky?' His fingers tightened in her hair, pulled her head back gently. 'Don't do this?' He whispered the words against her parted lips, seemed still to be speaking after the murmur died away. Warm, slow, soundless words tickled into her mouth and her lips answered them silently. He gathered her closer, his fingers rasping through her hair.

'Or don't do this?' He lifted his mouth to whisper against her cheek and then his lips trailed a hot, moist path down her throat. Behind her his hands kept pace, gliding down the back of her neck, down across her shuddering shoulders to slide around her waist and pull her still closer.

'Don't!'

'Don't what?' His whisper was laugh and caress all at once now. 'Don't kiss you here?' His lips moved against the base of her throat and she arched her back with a soft hiss. 'Or ... *here*?' The sheer fabric over her throbbing breast seemed to steam and then dissolve beneath his lips and his arms tightened around her till she gasped for air.

His back was warm and smooth as heated stone, and what were her hands doing there? Moving like that? Her body was tingling all over beneath the torrent of his lovemaking. His whispers seemed to come through the curtain of rain in her mind. They were falling through that rain, and only when her back sank into the cushions did she realise that it was really so. His weight and heat settled over her, electrifying, terrifying. 'Fletch, *don't*!'

A hand cupped her cheek, an unseen thumb stroked across her lips, and his low voice soothed above her. 'Don't be frightened, love. Don't be frightened.'

'Then don't frighten me!' she gasped, as his lips brushed her chin. Her hands found the wide shoulders above her and pushed helplessly. 'Please ... '

The dark room whirled dizzily and the weight lifted

from off her, but an arm still encircled her waist. Jolian found herself on top now, staring down into a dark face, half a smile barely seen. 'I'm sorry. Is this better?' His hand reached up to lace through the fall of her hair. 'You call the shots, then, General.'

Bracing her forearms on either side of him, Jolian tried to shut out the feel of her breasts against his hair-roughened chest, tried to remember who she was and why. For there would be no more chances tonight. And she would *not* wake up with a stranger. Not even such a stranger as this . . . 'All . . . right. Shot . . . Shot one: I offered you a couch tonight, Mr McKay, not a lay.'

The half-smile below her became whole, and a hand caressed slowly across her hips. 'I guess I was taking the broad interpretation . . . my mistake. And shot two?'

'Shot two: you're old enough to be my father!'

'The devil I am!' The arm around her waist tightened ominously. 'How old are you, brat?'

'Twenty-five.'

'Then I'm barely twelve years older than you!'

'And I bet you landed running! As I said, old enough to be my father.'

He laughed and his fingers slithered slowly up her spine. 'And shot three, you silky infant?'

'Shot . . .' Jolian swallowed hard, fighting the urge to simply melt down against him like a sun-warmed candybar. 'Shot three: I *don't* make love with perfect strangers, no matter what it looks like.'

She felt his laughter rumbling through her clenched stomach muscles. 'Then you've been missing out on a world of fun, you little puritan. And shot four?' His arms slipped slowly up around her raised shoulders.

'I . . .' She didn't have a shot four.

His arms tightened suddenly and he crushed her down against him. His mouth met her parted lips in a kiss that seemed to burn right through her. A full and smoking broadside of heated shot. A throbbing, deafening, twenty-one-gun salute. 'Shot four,' he laughed huskily, as he released her at last.

Jolian bounced off the couch like a scalded cat and raced for her room. No one pursued her and she whirled in the hall doorway, hair and silk robe flaring around her, her lips parting.

But Fletch was aiming forefinger and thumb in an imaginary pistol at her. 'Sleep on it!' he rapped out.

Shutting her teeth with a snap, she whirled away again, flung down the hall and then stopped, leaned panting against her bedroom doorknob. Why had she come out here in the first—*oh!* She spun around. 'And shut those damn windows!' she hissed.

The low, mocking voice came back faintly. 'Right you are . . . General.'

She didn't slam the door. Quite . . .

CHAPTER THREE

IT was ten a.m. Couldn't be, but it was. Yaffa crouched before the door in an intense ball, as if it would open any second now to her feline brainwaves. Jolian shut her eyes again, shutting out daylight and abused cat, tried not to remember.

But with no luck. Those fingers, those lips, that voice were stamped into her brain, branded across a body that even now stretched in its own voluptuous, yearning memory at the thought of last night. Oh damn, it wasn't supposed to happen like this!

It's the double-fudge sundae factor all over again, she told herself bitterly. *The nicest things in life are no good for you. And this one's pure poison. This man is trouble. Trouble, Jolian Michaels. For once in your life, be smart.*

Yaffa must have caught the change in her breathing. A light weight bounced on the mattress beside her. Whiskers brushed her cheek with a feather touch and a cool whiff of tuna. 'Yuk!' Jolian pulled the sheet over her head.

Those lips, that touch ... trouble. How do you trouble me, Fletcher McKay? Let me count the ways: Wrong values—work and money and work. Divorced, I think. If yes, he's a one-time loser. If no, well, just forget it. Too old. Too experienced. And much, much, much too fast. What had he said last night? That if she didn't sleep with strangers, she was missing a world of fun? Obviously, *he* had no such qualms. Not a shy lad, no. And what had Jem said? If he wasn't at the office, he'd be at Jennifer's, Barbara's or somebody's, that body being female? And no doubt every one of those females was trying every feminine wile in the book to

capture that heart as well as those hands and lips he
was so free with. No. If he wasn't caught by now, he
was not catchable. So forget it. Forget last night.

Might as well try to forget your own name. She
pushed the cat off and got up.

Except for the leather bag and briefcase tucked in a
corner by the sofa, Fletcher McKay might have been a
dream, stirring and strange and gone with the sunlight.
Jolian surveyed the room carefully, half expecting him
to pounce from some corner, but she was alone. The
feeling was not as pleasing as she would have thought.

A folded paper on the counter caught her eye.
Fletch's handwriting was large and bold, a nervy,
slashing line, not a businessman's scrawl at all. 'Glad to
know you're a woman who likes beds. Will stop back
later—we still have to talk. Dinner is my treat
tonight.—Fletch.'

Not 'will you have dinner with me,' but 'dinner is my
treat'. It figured. If he were the pirate he looked, he'd
not be sailing as first mate. The man liked to give the
orders, that was sure.

'Well, I have other plans, *Mister* McKay.' Jolian
folded the note into a paper aeroplane and aimed it at
the briefcase. Just what those plans were, she didn't
know yet, but she did know that one Fletcher McKay
would not figure among them. There must be some way
to dent that man's insufferable ego. The plane pulled a
low, lazy swoop, stalled out on the upturn, and crashed
tail first to the rug. Yaffa picked a stealthy, roundabout
path towards it, tail-tip flicking. Oh, yes, she did have
plans, come to think of it—George and the French
restaurant. An oddly deflating thought.

The day was oddly deflating as well. Jolian worked
on her designs in fits and starts, but her concentration
and her work were under par. Vacuuming, laundry, and
other chores filled the gaps between designs, but busy as
she stayed, she found herself pausing each time

footsteps climbed the stairs. And when the phone rang
at last, she ran for it. But it was only Hannah Bernstein,
with the news that Suzie's parents from Springfield had
just collected the girl and she had left smiling. Parents
and child sent their thanks.

Well, that was good news at least. One for Jane.
Jolian hung the phone up with a smile, but that smile
slowly faded as her eyes fell on his luggage. Where *was*
he? And what time was it? Four? Time to get ready for
her date. And what to wear? Suddenly she had the
impulse to knock the socks off George Trumble. That
would show him. She didn't stop to analyse just which
him would be shown exactly what as she headed for the
bathroom and the rose-scented bubble-bath.

'A penny for your thoughts.'

George *would* say something like that, Jolian thought
as she watched the brandy swirling in her glass. She
looked up from under her lashes, smiled mysteriously
and said nothing. He would hardly care to know that
she was re-living the slow, engulfing fire of that last kiss
last night, or that it was the fiftieth time she'd done so
today! She tasted the brandy with a cat-like flick of her
tongue. That slow-burning glow inside . . . just so. That
was how it had felt last night . . .

'No, really, what are you thinking?'

He *would* insist. 'Oh, just about corporate law . . .
how . . . fascinating it sounds.' As fascinating as
preparing tax returns. Possibly as thrilling as raising
earthworms, but she doubted it. *And you're completely,
totally unfair*, she thought quickly, smillng up at him to
make up for it.

Across the table, George swallowed hard. 'I'm . . .
glad you think so, Jolian. And did I tell you how
beautiful you are tonight?'

Jolian nodded. Twice. So the softly swirling, sapphire
blue dress was a success, or perhaps it was her hair,

pinned up off her neck in a soft, sleek pattern of French braids, or perhaps it was the scent of roses . . . Anyway, she had knocked his socks off. She was suddenly sure she had no desire to see George Trumble without his socks.

Now Fletch McKay without his . . . socks . . . would be another matter entirely. She hid a wry smile in her brandy snifter. *Just ask him and I'm sure he'd be glad to show you, dope!* No, it was the fudge factor, all right. Exquisite at the time of eating, paid for in heartburn later. Now why couldn't she fall for George here, as wholesome and stolid as a plate of steamed carrots? She grinned in spite of herself.

'And who's that smile for?'

'Oh . . . my cat. I just remembered it's past her feeding time.'

'She can wait.'

'She can, but she doesn't wait quietly, and the neighbours complain.'

'All right, then. Waiter?'

On the drive home, she kept him on the topic of law. George waxed expansive as she murmured questions and exclamations at the proper intervals, and she had time to think. This would be her last date with George; it was far better to be lonely alone than lonely in company. He was a very nice guy, but . . .

A sudden wave of depression washed over her as they turned into her street. How many very-nice-guys-but had she met in her lifetime? What was wrong with her? The fault had to be hers. Other people found people to love and marry . . . Puritan, he'd called her. Perhaps perfectionist was a better label.

George insisted on walking her to her door, his arm around her waist, and they were half a step out of sync the whole way up. Jolian nerved herself for the coming kiss, tried to blot out last night's. The contrast would be brutal.

The envelope she had tacked to her door was gone. So Fletch had come by to collect his luggage and find her 'thanks, but no thanks for the supper' note. She hoped he'd remembered to leave the key on the table as requested. She fished her own keys out of her purse, but George took them from her.

'Allow me.' He paused expectantly.

Now was the point when she should invite him in for coffee. However . . . 'It's been a lovely evening, George. I enjoyed it.'

'It doesn't have to end yet . . .'

'Well, I have to feed my cat.' And why was Yaffa so quiet? Could Fletch have let her out? Surely not.

'I'll help you. Cats always love me.' His hands found her upper arms, massaged them nervously.

'Not this cat, George. And I'm awfully sleepy tonight, but thank you. It was a terrific restaurant.'

He took it with less grace than she had expected. His face was sullen as he pulled her forward, and she realised as the kiss grew wetter and hotter than she'd bargained for that he was going to make the most of it, if a kiss was all he had coming. 'Hey!' she protested softly, bumping back against the door.

'Jolian, you don't know what you do to me!' He crowded closer, and he was panting now.

'Hey, come *on*, George!' If this was a sample of what she did to him, she wanted no more. Wet, clumsy— *'Hey!'*

The door opened suddenly under her weight, flooding the landing with light, and cat fur brushed her legs. She would have fallen but for the grapple-hold George had on her. He blinked past her shoulder.

'I thought that was you knocking. Did you forget your key, Jolian?' The low voice was smooth as whisky, quietly amused.

'I——' She turned in George's loosened grasp, her fear of a moment ago sliding towards rage. How dared he——

But he had dared more. Leaning casually against the door frame, Fletch was dressed only in slacks, his wide, hairy chest still beaded from the shower, his dark hair damply combed. He smiled gently at George. 'Fickle little thing, isn't she? You wouldn't think she was in my arms last night, would you?'

Jolian drew a hissing breath. '*You . . .!*'

'*Uh*-uh.' He set a large finger across her lips. 'Not in public, love. Now say goodnight to the man.' He closed the door gently in her face.

'Who the hell was *that*?' George exploded.

'My father!' she snapped. One jerk was quite enough; two were intolerable.

'Your——' George let go of her and stepped back. 'Okay, Jolian, it's been interesting. See you around.' He handed her the keys, wheeled with magnificent dignity and stepped on Yaffa's tail.

'*Wow!*'

She had one glimpse of him, cream-coloured, kicking ball of fur wrapped around left ankle, and then he was gone. Cat curses, thumps, and some words that were not only unlawyerly but probably illegal echoed up the stairwell.

'George, don't hurt her!'

Behind her, Fletch let out a whoop of pure bliss. 'Hurt *her*! You're heartless, lady!'

'*You!*' Jolian spun around. He stood in the doorway again, still bare-chested, head thrown back in laughter, and the target was irresistible. She whopped an open-fingered forehand into his stomach just as he laughed again. '*Ow!*' It was like hitting warm brick.

A hand slapped down over her bruised fingers, trapping them against that damp, muscular warmth. Narrow-eyed, he glared down at her. 'Watch it, sweetheart. I'm not your boy-friend.'

'I'll say you're not!' And there was no breaking that hold. His fingers merely tightened.

'As bad-tempered as your cat, aren't you?'

'Ya? . . . *Yaffa!*' Hand still trapped, she whirled back towards the stairs to see Yaffa gliding up the last step, ears laid back, chocolate tail enormous. Eyes flaming, she swept past their feet and disappeared. Down below, a door slammed, shaking the house.

'So she's okay. Are you?'

'No thanks to you!'

'Come on, Jolian, what was I supposed to do? You're twenty-five, though you look like a teenager who's just been pawed at the senior prom. Goddamnit, he cut you!' He dropped her hand and ran a quick finger under her bottom lip. 'No, just lipstick. Good, I'd never catch him now.'

She was past speech by now. He pulled her in gently and closed the door. She drifted across the room, noticed in passing that he'd taken over the table. The briefcase was open, papers stacked and scattered; a cup of coffee and a gold pen lay waiting. Made himself at home, hadn't he? She wandered on to her bedroom, wilted at the dressing table. Last night . . . tonight . . . everything seemed to be catching up with her at once . . .

In the mirror, her eyes were enormous and shadowed, the smooth hair a shambles. Behind her, Fletch pushed open the door and padded in, carrying two glasses of wine. He was still shirtless. Jolian opened her mouth and then shut it again. She should protest this invasion, but she hadn't the strength yet. And somehow the apartment, this room even, seemed to be his, not hers, tonight. He set a glass by her hand.

'Drink up. You need it.'

'Go to hell!'

'Later.' A large, gentle hand feathered across the top of her head as he stared down at her, smiling that half-smile. 'Must have been pretty once.' He tugged slowly at a loose pin. A curl untwisted and slid down her cheek. His hand caressed along her temple, found another pin, pulled it gently. 'When you're forty, Jolian, you'll look stunning with it up.' Another lock cascaded down her neck, and another. 'But at your age, I like it ... like this, all free and heavy ... something a man can bury his hands in.' He tossed the pins down on the table and picked up her hairbrush. 'Come on, drink up.'

Jolian heaved a deep sigh and drank. In a moment she would get up, throw him out. But he looked so big ... so unthrowable ... Through half-closed eyes, she watched those big rhythmic hands in the mirror. He was soothing her just like she soothed Yaffa, wasn't he? She drank again and listened to her hair crackle, resisted the pull of the brush with dreamy, slow nods. Any moment now she would be purring. *Wake up, Jolian.* 'Why ... why did you stay?' she asked.

'For two reasons.' Fletch put the brush down and buried his fingers in her hair, his fingertips moving in slow, rustling circles. 'I have to talk to you about Jem.' Slowly he pulled her head back to rest against his waist.

She leaned against him, hypnotised by the warmth, the sound, and the lovely sensations, her eyelashes drooping. 'And?' she breathed finally.

'And I wanted *this*.' The fingertips were gliding down now, slowly, so slowly. Smoothing her throat, warming her shoulders ... caressing just the very top of her breasts. Moving ever so deliciously slowly now. It was breathtakingly erotic, watching him touch her in the mirror at the moment she felt his touch. Her breasts were swelling, aching for him to gather them in, but his hands moved so slowly ...

Their eyes met in the mirror, hers heavy with desire, his almost black and gleaming, and he smiled, one eyebrow lifting. He was giving her time to say no. *Daring* her to say no.

Head tilted back, Jolian drew a deep, shaking breath, her breasts rising. His hands glided lower across the thin fabric of her dress, so slowly, the fingers stiffly outspread, the open palms at last finding, circling, caressing just the tips of her taut nipples. Deep in her throat, she purred, and the fingers closed gently over her breasts. *'Ohhh ...'* She arched her back slowly and he made a deep, half-laughing, male sound.

Wake up, Jolian. Wake up. Her eyes fluttered open and closed again. 'Are you seducing me, Fletcher McKay?' she murmured dreamily.

His fingers slid slowly, so slowly, up the slopes of her breasts, climbed the peaks, danced slowly there, melting her. 'Want me to? I'm very good at it.'

Funny how words could hurt. Why should that hurt? She lifted her head slowly, found those dark eyes waiting for her in the mirror above that faint, reckless smile. 'No ... thanks.'

His fingers stopped and the smile faded. 'No?'

Somehow she found the strength to find his hands, lift them away. 'No.'

His eyes narrowed and she swallowed hard as she met his gaze. He picked up his glass and wheeled away. In the mirror she watched him toss off the wine, shrug and turn back to her. 'So let's talk, then.'

She shook her head. 'Please, Fletch, I can't talk now. I want to sleep.'

A large hand smoothed down the line of her jaw, brushed her bottom lip with a butterfly touch. 'Then let's sleep together. We can talk later.'

'Sleep! Ha!'

His finger traced the shape of her mouth and he smiled. 'Well, we can sleep later, too.'

She nipped his thumb as it slipped between her lips and then jerked her chin aside. 'Thanks, but no, thanks.' She stood up quickly, felt the room lurch for a moment and then steadied herself. *Got* to get him out of here! She ducked around his outstretched hand and headed for the living room.

Pack him up and get him out of here! She collected the papers on the table, stacked them neatly into the briefcase. But an arm encircled her from behind, pulling her back against the warmth of his hard body. 'Why won't you let me make love to you?' He breathed the words in her ear and she shuddered.

'Because I ...' Jolian stopped, breathing deeply, trying to remember why.

'Because you don't make love with strangers?' His lips brushed across her hair and his arm tightened. 'If I keep coming round like this, I won't be a stranger much longer.'

She shivered and turned it into a headshake. 'Because you're not serious.'

His laughing whisper rasped her ear. 'Oh, silky one, you don't know how serious I am! Give me the night and I'll show you.' His lips found the top of her shoulder and she arched her back convulsively, pressing back against him.

'I'm ... looking for someone who'll ... show me the rest of his life, Fletch,' she gasped.

She felt his sigh as much as heard it. The arms around her loosened slowly. 'Well, maybe you'll find him some day, sweet silky ... maybe. But he's not here tonight.' He nuzzled her hair, brushed it aside as he searched for the nape of her neck. 'So what about tonight?'

It would hurt if she stopped to think. Hurt dreadfully. She twisted in the circle of his arms to face him. 'Tonight?' She tried to smile. 'Do you think you can find your way back to the Pussycat Lounge, or shall I draw you a map?'

His breath hissed in silent laughter, but his eyebrows came down. 'I don't want that, Jolian. I want you.'

She shook her head quickly and drawled out the words, a feeble joke. 'Well, you caaaan't *have* me!'

'Is that a fact?'

'That's a fact, Fletcher McKay.'

His arms tightened again. 'Only on my sufference is that a fact, you silky puritan.'

She'd got her hands up against his chest this time. Jolian pushed off, creating a little breathing space between them. 'Are you threatening me, Mr McKay? You've forgotten my man-eating cat,' she said breathlessly.

'Ask that cat who fed her tonight, and no, I'm not threatening violence. There's easier ways.' He pulled her closer, smiling dangerously.

'Stop!'

'Then admit it. You know I can have you whenever I want.'

'The hell you can!'

'The hell I *can't*! Want a demonstration?' One hand slid gently round to cup her breast. A slow, merciless thumb-flick brought her to bow-tight, quivering tautness in his hold.

'No!' she gasped, eyes clenching tight. '... *please*, Fletch.'

His thumb stroked again and again as he gathered her closer. 'Then grant me one wish,' he demanded huskily.

'... mmph?'

'Have breakfast with me. We've got to ... talk ... maybe it'll be easier in a restaurant than ... here.'

'*Ohhh* ... kay.' Anything to stop that sweet torture.

'*That's* better. Sure you want me to go?'

If she opened her eyes, he'd see the truth. She kept them closed.

Slowly he let her go, leaned her back gently till her hips found the edge of the table. She leaned back, breathing deeply, listened to the sounds as he gathered his papers, buttoned on a shirt, came to stand before her again. 'You're sure you want me to go, Jolian?'

Eyes shut, she nodded.

'So you can lie after all. I'll remember that.' A hand cupped her jaw and he kissed her, a slow, hungry, lingering kiss. 'I'll pick you up at eight, then.'

Blindly, she nodded again. Slow footsteps, a door closing gently, the stairs squeaking softly as he descended. 'Don't go,' she whispered. '*Please* don't go.'

CHAPTER FOUR

'GONE. Better luck next time—J.'

That should fix him. Promises made under duress were not binding at all, as far as Jolian was concerned. She taped the note to her mailbox in the downstairs hallway and stopped to consider it, frowning. This was not her usual style. This was cowardice, leaving a note and bolting. But Fletch scared her, or rather her response to him last night scared her. She shivered suddenly, remembering those warm, practised hands gliding across her body. Yes, he could have had her last night, and no, she would *not* fall for someone like Fletch McKay.

She'd fallen for the wrong man once before, her second year in college, had thrown herself into that affair with all her usual intensity and energy, certain that here at last was the solution to nineteen years of loneliness.

She grinned suddenly, remembering Rob's handsome, petulant face. Some solution! The only thing they had had in common was their admiration for Rob Collins, painter and lover. He hadn't needed her, he'd needed a full-length mirror equipped with doormat. Jolian laughed and shook her head. The inconceivable tastes of nineteen-year-old innocents!

Well, it was laughable now, but the year-long affair had been painful, more than painful, while she lived it. She had come away from that fiasco with a healthy respect for the heartache that misplaced love could bring and a cool determination never to waste herself on the wrong man again. The next time she loved, she would do it right.

So, after Rob, she had measured each suitor with an unblinking objectivity which perhaps had been as self-defeating as her first uncritical, headlong rush into love. In the years since, she had found many men to like, not one to love.

'Better luck next time.' Jolian found herself re-reading her note and frowned. Shouldn't have said that. She *didn't* wish him better luck—not with her anyway—she wished him gone. And she'd best be going too, but that note needed something . . . She fished a pen out of her shoulder bag and added a quick sketch—a Cheshire Cat with a sassy, defiant grin and one eye winking. There . . .

'Some artist,' Fletch commented behind her, his half smile lifting as she spun around. 'I'd expected better of you than that.'

Jolian caught her breath and pushed off from the mailboxes. 'You bring out the worst in me.'

'Glad to hear it's mutual.' A large hand closed around her upper arm and he started for the door. 'Let's go—I'm starving.'

Jolian dug in her heels, half tripped as he kept on moving, and followed unwillingly. 'What are you *doing* here, Fletch? It's only seven o'clock. You said eight!'

'And that's why I came at seven,' he said easily, his mouth twitching. He pulled her out into cool morning sunlight and started for the car parked across the street.

Jolian jerked against his hand again, shook her hair back in frustration. 'To quote a friend of ours—leggo!'

'In a minute.' In spite of his faint smile, there was a tightness around those deepset eyes, at the edges of those chiselled lips, that spoke of temper under tight control. Jolian hoped fiercely that he'd slept no better than she had. He opened the left front door and swung her on to the seat. 'In.'

Jolian blinked at the steering wheel. 'I'm driving?'

'No. Scoot over.' And he was quick. He was in the

car before she got the far door unlocked. He caught her
wrist and pulled her back. 'Don't try it.'

'Then don't try *me*!' she flared.

'Mmm . . .' He laughed suddenly, looking down at
her. 'Shall I say it?'

'Creep!' She turned her head away. Fletch lifted her
hand and kissed the palm. 'Mean-tempered little cat!'
He started the car and collected her hand again.
'Anyway, I'm glad to see you slept no better than I did.'

'I didn't say that.'

'You didn't need to. But maybe breakfast will help.'

Maybe it would. Jolian leaned back against the seat
and heaved a sigh. She'd run from him all night
through her dreams, woke up prepared to run some
more. It was almost a relief to be caught . . .

His hand squeezed her fingers and released her.
'That's better.'

And he would have to behave himself in public, after
all. Perhaps there was nothing here to fear but fear itself.
Besides, she had no choice, had she? And all kidnappers
should be so darkly handsome. Rationalisation complete, she smiled in spite of herself. Well, it was too
lovely a day to worry. 'Where are we going?' she asked.

'Harvard Square. The police tell me it's the favourite
hangout of new runaways.' He swung the car warily
into the traffic of Mass Avenue, the main artery linking
Boston and Cambridge. 'In the meantime, help me keep
an eye out for Jem. With all these fast-food joints and
stores, this looks like a likely street as well.'

'I don't know what he looks like, Fletch!'

He flicked her a rueful smile. 'So you don't . . . Look
in the manila envelope on the back seat.'

The envelope contained a stack of Wanted posters.
That was the only way to describe the paper with the
boy's photograph at the top of the page, the reward and
information printed below. 'My God, Fletch, he's your
son, not a criminal!' Jolian exclaimed.

'And I want him back.' His eyes flicked past her, scanning the sidewalks on both sides of the busy street. 'If that's what it takes, so be it.'

Jolian studied the young face before her, a handsome—no, a beautiful child, blond and elfin, with wide, intelligent eyes. An exceptional face, and one that teased at her memory. Puzzled, she turned to study the man beside her.

The car stopped at a light and Fletch glanced down at the poster. 'That was taken a year ago, before he started to fill out. He's not quite so pretty now, thank heavens.'

'Pretty?' Jolian laughed softly. 'He's not pretty, Fletch, he's gorgeous! Not like you at all!' She flashed him a teasing smile.

But her gibe was not well taken. A nerve tightened and fluttered beneath his right eye for an instant as his lips hardened. 'No. He's not.' His gaze swept through her without stopping. 'Now suppose you help me look for him?'

'Okay.' Jolian turned to the window, frowning thoughtfully. And why had that bothered him so? Her eyes swept across the early-morning sidewalks, an older man striding home with his Sunday edition of the *Globe*, two young girls entering a bakery; no teenage boys in sight, gorgeous or otherwise. She glanced down at the poster again, studying Jem feature by feature now. A delicately tilting nose where Fletch's was straight; mischievous, triangular smile with lips of even width, not at all like that hard, chiselled mouth with the slightly fuller lower lip that was becoming all too familiar . . . 'What colour are his eyes?' she asked.

'As it clearly says on the poster, love—blue.' He swore suddenly and tires squealed as he braked the car. 'Sorry.'

'Sure.' Jolian put a casual hand up on the dash and left it there, frowned at the back of the bus which had stopped before them. Was Fletch like this every morning before breakfast? It was odd to feel that she knew him so well, when she really knew nothing about him at all. She turned quickly to look back at a trio of bedraggled boys slouched on the hood of a parked car. They looked like street kids, all right.

'No,' Fletch said quietly beside her. 'None of those is mine, thank God.'

Jolian grinned in spite of herself and looked down at Jem's picture again. That pale blond hair should be easy to spot. A blue-eyed blond . . . so he must take after his mother then. 'She must be very beautiful,' she murmured.

'She is.' Fletch's face was as expressionless as his voice.

And the emotion which stabbed through her was utterly unexpected. Jolian had a split second vision of a drill press driving a drill through sterling sheet stock—the razor-sharp, silver spiral curling up from the hole. She blinked, and took a slow, careful breath. Coffee . . . that was what she needed . . . that and some sense . . . 'I thought you were going to feed me? This kidnapping *is* on the continental plan, isn't it?'

His face slowly relaxed and a smile almost started. 'That's the bed and breakfast plan, isn't it?'

'I've had the bed already, thanks!' she told him hastily as his fingers captured her hand again.

Fletch laughed softly and lifted her hand to his mouth. 'Then I guess I'll have the breakfast!' He buried a set of excellent teeth in the soft skin at the base of her thumb and bit down gently.

'Help!' His grip tightened as she tried to pull away. 'Watch the road, you cannibal!'

Still nibbling, Fletch growled something unintelligible and stopped for a pedestrian. Crossing in front of them, the woman turned to smile her thanks. Her mouth dropped and she bustled away, head high.

'Brute!' He was using his tongue now and Jolian could feel the warm stroke of it down to her toes. This wouldn't do at all! 'Unhand me!'

'I'm trying.' He held her hand out before him and studied it. 'But you're tougher than you look.' He licked her again thoughtfully, his eyes on the traffic, his tongue travelling slowly from the centre of her palm to the tip of her forefinger. 'Intriguing taste, though, lady. My appetite's only whetted.'

'Fletch, you're going to wreck us!'

'True.' He nipped the tip of a finger—a sharp, delicious pain—and released her. 'Worse yet, we're not looking for Jem.' He frowned suddenly and swept the sidewalks with a fierce glance. 'And where the hell is Harvard Square?'

'We're here.' Jolian crossed her arms, tucking her hands safely out of sight. 'That's Harvard to the right, behind this wall.' They passed a gate just then and she caught a glimpse of tall, dark brick buildings, slate roofs, ivy turning bronze and scarlet beyond the wrought iron lace. 'It's not a formal square really, just a place where several streets intersect.'

'And what's its attraction?' He slowed the car to a crawl as they passed a group of youngsters on the corner, then drove on, frowning again.

'Oh, it's just a district with lots of boutiques and cafés and bars that's grown up around the college. I suppose it's a good place to panhandle too.'

His breath hissed as he stopped to let the van ahead back into a slot at the kerb. 'I don't know what I'd do if I found Jem begging on the street. It would be a toss-up whether I hugged him or whether I just kicked his young rear all the way to Chicago!'

Jolian studied the muscles tensed along the clean line of his jaw. 'I think you'd better hug him, Fletch,' she said dryly.

His brows came down dangerously and then relaxed

again and he nodded, staring blindly as the driver made a second attempt to fit into the space. He sighed and suddenly leaned back against the headrest to stare up at the overhead. 'God, yes,' he muttered bleakly. His breath hissed in an angry sigh and he shut his eyes.

It was suddenly necessary to touch him. Without thought Jolian reached out, ran a gentle finger along that tensed eyebrow.

His lips quirked for an instant but he shook his head. 'Don't make me feel good, Jolian. I need to feel bad,' he said softly. 'Very bad.'

'True.'

His smile was wry this time. The car behind them honked. He shot a savage look over his shoulder and started them moving again.

'When did you last hug him?' she asked gently.

'July.' He shook his head again. 'July ... *God!*' He laughed a bitter, soundless laugh. 'And I was going to be everything to Jem that my father wasn't to me!'

Jolian resisted the impulse to touch him again. 'What wasn't he to you, Fletch?'

'Around!' he bit out. 'Now where the hell do we park?'

'Take a left up ahead.' She eyed him cautiously. How far could she pry before he lashed out at her? 'He didn't have time for you?'

'You might say that.' Following her point, Fletch swung the car into the municipal parking lot. 'He walked out the door one day, when I was about nine, and forgot to come back again.'

'Oh.' Jolian had a ridiculous need to put her arms around him and hug him, as if that could somehow heal a wound inflicted before she was even born. While she fought that urge, Fletch parked the car, his face set in a tough half-smile which warned her not to try it. She was still frowning absently into space when he opened her door.

'You coming?'

'Oh . . . sure.' She swung long legs out of the car and stood up to find herself toe to toe with him. The man didn't back down very well. And short of sitting down again, there was no retreat. She looked up into those green-gold eyes with a haughty surprise that belied what her heart was doing as his hands found her shoulders. But indignation hadn't helped much in the past, had it? Perhaps distraction was the answer. 'What was he like?' she asked quickly as he swayed her forward. She caught her balance with a hand against his chest, her arm stiff.

Fletch's mocking half-smile faded. Just as she decided that he wouldn't answer that, he spoke. 'He was good with his hands. A carpenter . . . and a damn good one. I hear he was good with the women as well.' His hands tightened and the smile reappeared, but the mockery was for himself now. 'A lot like me, I suppose.'

Jolian caught his wrists and lifted his hands away— was relieved that he allowed this. She held them up before her face and inspected them, frowning judiciously. '*You* don't work with your hands.' She slipped under his arm and moved away, then stopped to look back, smiling now that she was free again.

The remark seemed to nettle him. 'I did once.'

'What happened?' She buried her hands in the pockets of the heavy cardigan she'd thrown over a red cotton shirt and slacks this morning, but it was no use. Fletch slipped his hand through her arm and took her in tow. Frowning, she hung back. He shortened his stride, but didn't let go. 'What happened?' she repeated.

'I just decided I could make more money other ways.'

'And money's important?' She studied his chest from the corner of her eye. He had changed the elegant businessman's suit for some snug, well-worn jeans and a light sweater. But the brown leather jacket he had slung over one shoulder gave his outfit the lie if you looked at it closely. Leather with that buttery, supple look cost money. Lots of it.

'Oh yes, it's important.' He stopped them at the corner and glanced down at her, one eyebrow lifting. 'Now where for breakfast?'

'This way.' Jolian tugged gently and he followed her across the busy street. 'Funny,' she murmured, as they sauntered past the small shops offering books, music, pizza, dry-cleaning—all the needs of a college populace, 'funny, but I've never thought it was all that important.'

'That's what they all say, Puritan.' His arm tensed to match the words, crushing her arm against his side for a moment. 'But when push comes to shove, or rather, when supper comes down to baked beans three times in a week, they sing another song.' He dropped her arm suddenly and glanced down at her, smiling that cool, tough, meaningless smile she was learning to hate. 'So where's this restaurant?'

'We're nearly there.'

But when she led him into the small café on a side street, he looked around, frowning. 'You couldn't think of any place fancier?'

Jolian slid into a booth and smiled up at him. 'Sure, there are fancier places, Fletch. But none with better omelettes. Do you mind?'

His half smile was genuine this time as he sat across from her. 'No. I just thought you might like something special.'

'This *is* special. You'll see.' And this morning and this man were special too, Jolian realised as she studied his face bent over the menu in the honeyed light coming in at the window. He looked up suddenly and their eyes locked. Jolian took a deep breath. Careful ... Distraction, that was the idea ... but distract whom? 'Answer me a question?'

Those green-gold eyes stroked her face, warming it, or was that just sunshine? 'If you'll answer me one.'

'Okay—mine first. How did you find me?'

Fletch's faint smile was teasing. 'It's easy enough to trace a call, if you know when it's coming, provided you can keep the nitwit on the line long enough! That's when I knew for sure that you weren't a kidnapper!'

Jolian scowled. 'And how did you get here so fast?'

'That's two questions . . .' He studied her face with amusement, then glanced up as the waitress arrived with a fragrant coffee pot.

'So, I'll give you two,' Jolian offered recklessly as she passed him the cream.

'Fair enough. I had my bag packed, and a Lear jet chartered and waiting at O'Hare. All I needed was a destination, and you provided that.' Fletch took a long, appreciative sip of his coffee, then put the cup down, his dark eyes intent, his smile gone. 'Now, my turn.'

'Yes?' She shifted uneasily before that searching gaze, but couldn't break it.

'I had some time to look around your apartment last night, and it's very nice—too nice for a jewellery-maker. So where do you get your money? Is someone keeping you there? And if so, where is he?'

It took a moment to catch her breath. 'That's three questions, and they're all three obnoxious!'

'And that's not an answer'

The waitress chose that moment to break their clashing gaze with two lightly browned omelettes, steaming and puffed high with mushrooms and ham. Jolian smiled automatically and clutched at her temper with an effort. 'First of all, Fletch, I'm not a jewellery-maker, if by that you mean someone who makes earrings and peddles them from a pushcart. I'm a jewellery *designer* and I own half of one of the best design studios on the East Coast—*I* think in the country. We're new, but we're on our way up. Our work has been featured in *Craft Horizons*, in *Modern Jeweler*, and in *Vogue* in the last two years. We provide all the designs worn on all the televison series produced by Jacob Stine. We provide a lot of jewellery to a lot of the better galleries and department stores on this coast and a few in California . . .' True as this all was, it began to sound like bragging. She shut her mouth and sliced into her omelette.

'Well, well!' Fletch studied her for a moment, his half-smile appraising but not unkind. They ate in prickly silence, then settled back for a second cup of coffee.

'And who is your partner?' he asked at last.

'A friend of mine from college—Al Frasier. Al handles the production end of the business. We do some of the work in house, but some of the processes, like casting and enamelling, we job out to local factories. Then I handle the creative end—the designing. And we have three full-time salespeople around the country who market our lines.'

'And this Frasier,' Fletch asked quietly, 'is he your lover?'

The man was insufferable! Did he think of nothing else? 'What if he were? What's it to you?'

Slow and warm as a touch, his green-gold gaze roamed across her face and shoulders, lingered on her breasts stirring beneath the thin shirt and came back to her face. His almost-smile deepened. 'Only that if he is, silky, I intend to replace him.'

Jolian's fingers trembled with some emotion, arousal or rage, she wasn't sure which. She clenched them around her coffee mug and sipped deliberately, her eyes narrowed and blazing at him above the rim. She licked a stray drop off her lip with the tip of her tongue. 'I told you last night, Fletch, I'm looking for a permanent love, not a one-night . . . or a one-month . . . or a one-year affair. And that's all you're offering, isn't it?' In spite of herself, she held her breath.

His smile had disappeared now, leaving a molten

gaze that was both promise and challenge. 'Yes.'

It wasn't fair, wasn't fair, wasn't *fair*! And the emotion bubbling within her was rage. 'So what more do I need to say?' She lowered the mug carefully, smiled a brilliant, savage smile. 'Case dismissed.'

'Oh, really?' he whispered.

The frustation rushing through her had to find release. Her head came up and her eyes widened. It was throw something or cry. But his hand shot out to grip the other side of her mug even as the thought formed, and they glared at each other, fingers touching.

So that left only tears. She left him holding the mug and bolted from the table, swooped past the startled faces in the other booths and out of the door. The sunshine hit her smack in the face, radiant through the tears. Stunned, she stumbled to a halt and rubbed her eyes, then started out again.

'Just a minute!' An arm encircled her, yanked her back against his chest. 'What's the matter, Jolian?'

'Mister!' The worried voice of their waitress called from the doorway just behind them. 'Don't you want your change?'

'Keep it.'

'But it's——'

'*Keep* it.' His arm tightened as Jolian tried to pull away and he gave her a shake. 'What's the matter? Why are you crying?' His lips brushed the back of her neck.

The anger was slowly seeping away, she used the last of it to hold herself rigid in his arms. 'I always cry when I'm angry,' she growled, 'don't you?'

She felt him laugh. 'Not recently.' He kissed her ear and let her go. She moved off, but not alone. A pair of large shoes kept time with her own boots as she stalked along, her eyes downcast, her fists jammed in her pockets. 'And where do you think you're going?' he asked.

To the subway to catch a train. She'd collect her bike and then perhaps go and cry on Al's shoulder. Or go and walk by the river. Or drown herself. Maybe she'd go to the Museum and visit the Egyptian collection again ... '*Else*where!'

'Hey, very good.' She looked up as Fletch pulled her to a halt beside a lamp-post. From the tattered posters and handbills plastered to the silver column, a blond, grinning boy looked down at them—Jem.

'When ... when did you put this up, Fletch? Yesterday?'

He shook his head, staring back at his son, a quizzical, almost bewildered smile on his lips. 'I didn't.'

'Then how ...?'

'It's called delegation of responsibilities, infant.' Fletch collected her arm and nudged her away from the pole. 'I spent yesterday talking with the police, and then tracking down an investigator. Looks like I hired the right man.'

'An investigator?'

'Mm-hmm. Someone to do the legwork, or to see that it's done. I want this city plastered with those posters. I want one in every emergency room in every hospital, one in every clinic in the city. I want someone who can patrol the likely hang-outs when I'm not in town, who can make the rounds of all the shelters that might take him in ...'

'You're hunting him down like some criminal!'

Fletch shook his head, his eyes hard. 'You know as well as I do, Jolian, what an ugly world this can be. There's more ways to exploit a child than Jem has ever dreamed of, and he may be smart, but he's about as street-wise as a golden retriever pup. And his mother gave him three hundred dollars to get home on.' His lips twisted bitterly. 'There are people in this town who would knife him for five ...' He stopped as the pavement opened out into the small bricked square of

Holyoke Center, his eyes scanning the crowd gathered around a pair of chess players who faced each other cross-legged across a mammoth chessboard.

Jolian eyed the bent heads of the browsers at the pushcarts, focused on a couple perched laughing on the knee-high kerb enclosing the square's pocket garden. But no, that blonde was a girl ... Kids walking, kids talking, a couple necking on the long concrete bench that bounded the square, not a one of them Jem ... 'And what if you alienate him completely, Fletch, chasing after him with bounties and detectives?'

'That's a chance I'll have to take.' Fletch broke his search to glance down at her. 'The first thing is to get him off the street. After that, I'll try to make amends ... a lot of amends.' His eyes turned back to the square.

'And what will you buy him first?'

He smiled absently. 'I thought I'd get him a——' His brows came down as he turned to look at her. 'Is that supposed to be a joke?'

She tried to hold it back for a second, then threw back her head as the laughter pealed out. He was hopeless! And his kiss caught her just as she gasped for air. It was more exciting than oxygen, but not so useful. Blue sky and sunlight imploded into dark, moving warmth, the feel of his lips. And where was up? Clutching at his neck just as he released her, she hung there, panting. He was chuckling, damn him!

'That'll teach you ... hey, are you all right?'

'Dizzy ...' she muttered firmly.

'Right. Over here.' Arm around her waist, he guided her somewhere. The darkness was receding again, their feet and the pavement visible now at the centre of a widening circle. He turned her gently. 'Sit.'

The concrete bench was cold beneath her thighs. Fletch sat beside her and the arm he wrapped around her shoulders was deliciously warm. She leaned her head back and found his green-gold eyes just above her. '*Oh*, no!'

His arm tightened. 'Sit still, idiot, or I *will* do it again. That's the best reaction I've ever got. Or do you do that often?'

'It's nice to breathe,' she told him. And no, it had never been like that before, not with Rob, not with anyone. This was the most dangerous man she'd ever met! 'I've got to go.'

'Not just yet. I've a proposition to make.'

'I've heard it.' Through his sweater, she could feel the strong, steady rhythm of his heart. She took a deep breath, but the clean, masculine scent of him made her dizzy again.

'No, this is a different one, though that one still stands.'

Jolian shrugged her shoulders, but shuddered suddenly at the feel of her arm rubbing against the muscled warmth of his chest.

His arm tightened in automatic response. 'This one is strictly business, Jolian. If you can talk Jem in for me, I'll give you double that reward.'

Double . . . Jolian calculated mechanically. 'Talk him in?'

'If he calls you back again, I want you to persuade him to meet you someplace. I'll be waiting there.'

She twisted around to face him. 'Ever eaten ten thousand dollars before, Mr McKay? I hear it's tastier than thirty pieces of silver.'

'Jolian, I'm serious.'

'And so am I serious, Fletch! I'm not going to betray that kid.' She looked up at him pleadingly. 'Don't ask.'

'But I *am* asking.' His eyes were pitiless, as if he could bend her to his will with the heat of that molten gaze. 'For his own good.'

She shook her head. 'It's never for your own good, to

be lied to by someone you trust. I won't do that, Fletch.' She tried to stand up, but the hand on her shoulders tightened brutally.

'You damned little righteous puritan!' He stared down at her savagely. 'I forgot to tell you where else I'm sending a poster.'

Against her arm, his heart was thumping now like some animal leaping against the bars of its cage. If that beast should ever break free ... She licked dry lips. 'Where?'

'The morgue, Jolian, and God help you if I find Jem there ...' His free hand found her throat, caressed her with a velvety, measuring touch.

Rage, fear, pity, the feel of his hand on her bare skin—for a moment she couldn't speak. Perhaps if you drank boiling champagne, would it feel like this? She found her voice. 'Don't put your guilt on me, Fletcher McKay! *I'm* not the one who neglected him!'

'Neglect? He said *that?*' Fletch was on his feet, yanking her up beside him. He wrapped an arm around her waist and wheeled her towards the side street.

'Where are we going?' she demanded.

'We're going to walk so I don't throttle you! Now tell me everything he said. Start at the beginning and give me *everything*, Jolian, every word, every tone, every background noise ... and if you say the word "confidential" just *once*, I'll break your neck!'

'And so, do you think he'll call back?' The furious march had gradually slowed to a thoughtful pacing as Jolian talked, and now their steps hit the sidewalk in slow, perfect time. They had walked to the river under trees just beginning to catch fire, and Fletch had picked one flaming maple leaf. She had declined to eat it, so he had tucked it behind her ear. Now they were nearing the square again.

'I told you, Fletch, I just don't know.' Jolian stopped

them in front of a gallery window to inspect the
jewellery with professional interest. Nothing to get
excited about ... Her eyes lit on a modernistic rocking
chair just beyond, obviously a handmade, one-of-a-
kind piece. She'd once thought of becoming a
furniture designer ... 'Look at the rocker, Fletch! It's
lovely.'

'Mmm,' he stared at it intently. 'But he's used
Philippine mahogany. I've always hated that wood.' He
gave a sort of shake and tugged her away from the
window, his face set.

She glanced up at him curiously. 'What's wrong with
it?'

'Nothing, really ... it's easy to work with. But it
rarely has decent colour and I don't like to stain ...'
His breath hissed suddenly and he stopped.

She turned to study his face. 'You know, I don't even
know what you do.'

His half-smile was mocking, almost bitter. 'Sell
furniture.'

'Furniture?' It was the last thing she'd have guessed.
Rum-running, gun-running, importing cocaine, maybe,
but ... furniture? 'You mean like that piece?'

Fletch snorted soundlessly. 'I mean like white wood.'

'White wood?'

'Unfinished furniture, kitten. Cheap bookcases,
cheap desks, cheap tables, cheap whatever the customer
wants in cheap pine. No glamour, but lots of money for
me.'

'And money's important,' she murmured thoughtfully.

'Damn right.' He ground out the words.

She could feel each one of his fingers biting into her
waist now. 'You actually do the selling?'

Fletch laughed shortly and the fingers eased a little.
'Not exactly. I own the stores—I let others sell it.'

'Stores?'

'Eleven in four States now.' There was a kind of rueful pride in that answer. 'And more to come.'

'I see.' But she didn't. Why did he hate it so, or why do it if he hated it? 'How long have you been doing that?'

'Nearly eight years.'

Eight years . . . She made a sudden guess. 'And when did you and your wife divorce?' She felt his fingers jerk into her waist and then relax carefully.

'About eight years ago.' The words were casually offhand. Fletch glanced around suddenly, taking his bearings. They were on the corner across from the news stand and the subway station. 'Want some coffee yet?' It was a definite change of subject.

'No, I've got to go now.' It was all too intense. She had too much to think about. Eight years . . . She was suddenly exhausted.

'Go?' Fletch frowned down at her, his fingers stroking her ribs through her shirt. 'Don't go. I could use your eyes while it's light, Jolian. Once the sun goes down we'll have an early dinner someplace special before I catch my plane.'

'You're going back to Chicago?' And the pain that this brought was an unmistakable warning. This man was *trouble*. Trouble like she'd never dreamed before.

'Yes.' His green-gold eyes searched her face. 'This couldn't have happened at a worse time. I'm in the middle of a deal . . .'

'And we've got to keep things in perspective, don't we?' she cooed. 'First things first, right? Business now, sons later.' And no time for love at all.

'Damn it, Jolian, I can't just drop it. I'll tie up some loose ends and be back as soon as I can.'

'Fine. In the meantime I'm going. Thanks for breakfast.'

But he pulled her back again, his eyes raking her face. 'And just where are you going?'

Jolian shrugged and smiled. She hadn't thought that far yet. But it was necessary to be gone. The whole day had been a dreadful mistake . . . Nothing to fear but fear itself—ha!

'To Frasier? Is that where you're going?' he asked savagely.

Yes, that was exactly where, she realised suddenly, to Quicksilver Studio to remind herself who she was—a competent, successful somebody; not some rag doll to be dragged around Harvard Square for Fletch's amusement—used now, cast off later when the next doll came along. 'Yes.'

But his arm tightened, forcing her up on her toes against him. And from the look on his face, the racing speed of his heart through the light sweater, this would not be a gentle farewell. His narrowed eyes seemed enormous and she watched them shift from her lips, to her nose, to her eyes in a leisurely catalogue. Through their thin clothing, their hearts were renewing acquaintanceship, searching for and finding the same beat, a jam session in double time. But Fletch's anger was fading, or at least going underground, as that cool, untouchable smile slowly lifted the corners of his lips. He dropped her abruptly. 'Fine. Tell him hello for me, silky.' He turned and walked away.

Flat-footed, thunderstruck, cheated of a kiss she hadn't wanted, Jolian glared after him, her hands clenched into fists. Fletch turned suddenly. 'I'll phone you Tuesday night,' he called, 'to see if you've heard from Jem.'

'And if—if—I'm home, I might even answer the phone. I might . . .'

For a hopeful, fearful second she thought he was coming back again. 'You'd better!'

'And you give my love to Jennifer and Barbara and Jo and Marina, will you?' She smiled brilliantly.

'Marisa. And as you don't want it, you bet your

sweet bottom I will!' His brows a dangerous, dark line, he took a step backward, ignoring the amused stares of the passers-by.

'You ... go ... to *hell*!' She had never been so mortified in all her life!

'Tuesday,' Fletch reminded her pointedly.

'*Now* would be nicer!' And there was no way to win a screaming match on the street. Face flaming, she turned and dodged across the traffic, stamped down the stairs to the subway. A blond, beautiful boy grinned at her from a poster on the damp wall. 'It's all *your* fault!' she told him bitterly.

CHAPTER FIVE

'Reachout Hotline.'

'You told him!'

'Jem?' But of course it was him. Jolian squeezed the receiver anxiously, her thankfulness shading quickly to guilt. 'Jem, listen——'

'You *promised* me, then you told him where I was!' The gruff young voice wavered dangerously for an instant, angry tears not far off, then became even angrier to hide the slip. 'You *told* him!'

'Jem, I did *not*!' Jolian shook her head firmly, her blue eyes distant and intense. 'I didn't. I swear by every last one of Ralph's whiskers, I didn't! By every baked bean in Boston I didn't!' She stopped for breath and then held it, waiting.

'By every baked bean?' he asked at last carefully, his voice caught between hostility and bemusement.

Jolian breathed silently and slid slowly down in her chair to gaze up at the ceiling. 'By every single solitary last one, Jem,' she assured him fervently. 'You can come count 'em if you don't believe me.'

'But ... those posters ... how did ...'

'He tricked me, Jem. He traced the phone call the second time I called him.'

'I *warned* you.' The irritation returned with a growl.

'Mmm, you warned me, Jem, but you didn't warn me enough. He's *murder*! How did you put up with him so long?' She grinned suddenly, picturing his father's arrogant, dark face. That really was a good question.

'It wasn't easy,' Jem confided gruffly.

'I bet ...' Jolian murmured with genuine sympathy. And somehow, suddenly, some invisible line had been

88

crossed. 'You better believe it,' he told her. 'You know he can smell a beer on your breath at fifty yards?'

'Oh, I believe it.' And she would remember it, too. 'He looks like one tough customer.'

'He is.' There was a son's pride, as well as a survivor's, in that agreement. 'So . . . where is he, right now, Jolian?'

'Chicago. He went back on Sunday, Jem.'

'Oh.' And there was just a trace of disappointment in that quiet word? Jolian waited. 'Did he say when he'd——'

'Jem,' she interrupted suddenly, 'we're not really allowed to use the phones to just chat. They're for messages.'

'Oh!' There was definitely hurt in the young voice this time.

She hurried on. 'Look, tomorrow is supposed to be a nice day, and we won't have too many more. I'm going to go sketch in the Public Gardens all afternoon. Why don't you meet me there, and you can buy me that cup of coffee you owe me?'

'I owe you a cup of coffee?' he squeaked. His following hiss of exasperation made her grin again.

'You sure do! Your old man put me through more grief in one weekend than I've had in the last five years.' *And that was no lie*, she thought wryly. 'He seemed to think I had you in my back pocket. The very least you can do is buy me a coffee for all my troubles.' A sudden thought occurred. 'Or. . . if you're broke, Jem, I'll buy you a coffee. Then you'll just owe me two.'

'I've got money,' he said stiffly. There was a long pause. 'So what do you look like, Jolian, and where will you be?'

'I'm medium height, Jem, with dark brown hair,' she told him gravely. 'I'll be wearing a long red velvet gown, and a white chicken on my head. I'll be eating a banana and reading the *New York Times . . .*'

He laughed, and it was a tenor echo of his father. 'Did anybody ever tell you you're crazy, Jolian?'

'Oh, I guess maybe a few hundred people have ... but what do *they* know?' They agreed on a time and place for the rendezvous and at last Jolian hung up.

She tucked up her legs and gave the chair a gleeful spin. Masculine pride, it worked every time! She'd hit just the right note, saying he owed her a coffee. The cloudy, grey day spun into view and her smile faded. If only his father were that easy to handle ... And perhaps she was counting her chickens with Jem too soon. He could always change his mind by tomorrow. Or it could rain ...

But the lavender clouds were shredding and streaming off to the east by the time Jolian pedalled home from the hotline office. Across the silver-blue river, the jagged brick pile of Beacon Hill glowed blood-red spangled with squares of fiery copper as its windows gave back the last of the sunlight. Tomorrow should be cool, but clear. And what in heaven's name was she going to tell Fletch about tomorrow, if he called? The man was perfectly capable of flying back here tonight, if he thought she could lead him to his son.

You tell him nothing, dope. Just don't answer the phone tonight, she told herself sternly. And there was no use admitting that the thought of Fletch returning tonight made her heart pirouette like a ballerina on catnip. No use at all. She pedalled faster, as if she could leave that thought behind her, spinning in the twilight.

But it was one thing to resolve not to answer the phone, and quite another to carry that resolution through, Jolian thought grimly as the phone started ringing again. This made the third time since she'd walked in the door. She shoved her chair back from the drawing table and then stopped herself. What time was it anyway? Eleven-thirty, by her watch. Surely he would give up soon. On the edge of the table, Yaffa stirred and lifted her sleek head. Pale blue eyes met dark blue above the pencilled roughs for a new bracelet. 'Answer the phone, Yaffa,' she instructed the cat. 'Tell the man I love him madly and to kindly go jump in the lake, would you?'

The cat considered her gravely, as if she believed this late-night drivel. The phone stopped.

'Good.' Jolian sighed and stood up. 'Bedtime,' she announced. As if she would sleep. She could feel Fletch's angry, insistent vibrations humming down the telephone wires from Chicago even in the silence, like the sensation of a pair of green-gold eyes boring into her spine. 'Leave me alone,' she growled, wandering out of the workshop.

But he didn't. The phone rang again just as her lids drooped in hard-won sleep at last.

This was too much. *Too much*, she told herself, stalking down the hallway. She snatched up the phone and held it to her ear, too irritated to speak.

'Jolian?' That whisky-smooth voice was unmistakable. It stirred the hairs at the nape of her neck as if his lips brushed her there. 'Are you there, love?'

'Mmm,' she murmured, smiling in spite of herself.

'And where the hell have you been, my silky cat? Out on the town?' Fletch breathed, the anger beginning to seep through the velvety tone.

Her anger reawakened to meet his. 'And what gives you the right to even ask?' she flared back.

'Let's just say I'm ... taking an interest,' he purred evenly. 'Did Jem call today?'

The change of attack caught her off guard. 'Ah——'

'So he did,' Fletch concluded.

'I didn't say that.'

'You didn't need to, silky. I can read you like a book. Can you imagine what we'll be like in bed together?'

'No!' she whispered.

'Liar. So I'll tell you then . . . We'll leave the lamp on, so I can watch your face, and I'll——'

'*Fletch!*'

He laughed softly. 'So what did he say?'

Jolian blinked. 'Who?'

'You talked with Jem. What did he say?'

'Oh . . . he was mad at me.'

'For the posters? I hope you two made it up.'

'Why?' She sank down slowly on the edge of the table.

'Because if anyone can coax that kid down out of the tree, I think it's you, Jolian. I'm counting on you.'

And there was the truth of the matter, the long and the short of it, she thought bleakly. She blinked her eyes rapidly and then scrubbed a rough hand across her lashes. Fletch thought she could recover Jem for him; *that* was the interest he had in her. Anything else he got from her would just be a nice little bonus to the business at hand.

'What are you wearing?' he murmured in her ear.

'Why?' she growled. And why couldn't he stay on one subject? She was beginning to feel like a ping-pong ball with Fletch waiting for her at both ends of the table!

'Because I'm undressing you in my mind, kitten.' His low voice was a laughing caress. 'It helps to know what I'm taking off.'

She shuddered violently, ghostly fingers stroking down her spine, and wrapped her robe more tightly around her. '*Damn* you, Fletch. Cut it out!'

'Is it that blue silky thing?' he insisted.

'Yes,' she hissed.

'Good,' he murmured in husky satisfaction. 'I thought so.'

'And good*night*, Fletch.' Why had she ever answered the phone? She'd never sleep now!

'Stay in touch with him for me, Jolian, will you?'

She sighed. 'I'll try.'

'Good girl. I'll be back in town in a few days . . . and, silky?'

'Yes?' she breathed reluctantly.

'Don't sleep in the middle of the bed tonight. I take up a lot of space——' His warm, laughing whisper was cut short as she slammed the phone down.

Jolian glanced down at her watch again and then continued sketching, frowning slightly against the bright afternoon sunlight. So maybe Jem wasn't going to show after all. She stopped again, sat tapping the butt end of the pencil against the pad, and stared across the duck pond towards the willow she had been drawing, picturing it for an instant as a graceful, sweeping bracelet in silver and the deep greens of cloisonné enamel. The imaginary greens lightened, spun into circles, took on flecks of sunny gold, and Jolian scowled in sudden recognition. *Go away*, she thought fiercely. Fletch had cost her enough peace of mind the night before, might just as well have shared the bed with her, for all the sleep she'd got . . . He *had* shared the bed, blast him. Go *away*!

She looked around quickly, wondering for a second if she'd spoken aloud. But no one was near. The groups of chatting women, the silent men with their newspapers had long since packed up their brown bags and their sandwich wrappings, had left their benches to trail back to their offices leaving the sun-warmed grass to an old man sleeping among the pigeons, a young mother teaching her child to walk, a couple sauntering hand in hand. The public garden snoozed again in the late September sunlight, its peace all the sweeter for the distant rumble of traffic beyond the wrought iron boundary fence. Above the tops of the reddening trees, the skyscrapers loomed like far-off mountains.

Jolian checked her watch again. An hour late. No, he wasn't going to show. As much of a nuisance as his

father. She sighed, more disappointed than annoyed.
Well, it served her right for not minding her own
business. This proposed rendezvous went far beyond
the duties of a hotline volunteer, after all. You weren't
expected to—couldn't—get this involved with every
waif who called the office. You'd be an emotional
wreck in no time.

But Jem had caught her interest from his first call
with his obvious intelligence, his whimsical 'peachy
keen', his devotion to Ralph. 'Cat lovers of the world,
unite,' she murmured wryly, beginning to shade in her
sketch with precise layers of cross-hatching. So many of
the runaways sounded like sad little losers, at least at
the moment they phoned the hotline. Jem had sounded
like a winner, the kind of little brother she'd always
wanted when she wasn't wishing for a little sister, years
ago ... No, apart from Fletch, she would have still
wanted to meet Jem, to help him if possible.

Apart from Fletch ... if you could say anything in
her life was apart from Fletch nowadays, damn him.
No, she'd be a liar if she denied that knowing Fletch, or
rather, *not* knowing the man, made her all the more
anxious to meet Jem.

Fletch hid himself so well behind that hard smile,
that cocksure sexual aggression. But surely his son, at
fourteen, would not be so well armoured yet. Whether
he wanted to be or not, Jem was a part of Fletch's life
and his blood, a product of his love. In meeting the
boy, she might gain a few more clues to the nature of
the man behind that polished mask.

Her pencil curved down the page, idly doodled a
sprawling, calligraphic T followed by r, o, u, b—Jolian
caught herself and looped the pencil up the paper to the
willow again, continued shading it determinedly. No
doubt about it, that man was trouble. Fletch was one
big walking heartache, looking for a girl to happen to.
Getting involved with Fletch would be a big mistake.

But did she have a choice any more? What had happened to all her cool objectivity where men were concerned?

Well, perhaps that was the real motive behind her eagerness to meet Jem. If she could just talk to the boy, persuade him to go back to Fletch somehow, then Fletch would go away, leave her alone before she made a fool of herself. Her stomach turned a slow, queasy somersault at that thought. Or more likely, it had just figured out it had missed lunch. She finished the willow and sketched in a few lines to suggest the banks of the pond and the tree's wavering reflection in the dark water lapping at its roots.

Or maybe she was sitting here because she'd hoped to make a gift of Jem to Fletch, just so she could watch him smile . . . This was *absurd*.

Jolian glanced at her watch again. Well, whatever she'd wanted from this meeting, she wasn't going to get it. Jem had stood her up. Might as well start without him. Closing the sketchpad, she reached into the bag on the bench beside her and pulled out a loaf of bread. As she ripped open the wrapper, a single white duck cruised out of the shadows below the bridge spanning the pond. Neck outstretched, he homed in on the crust she tossed, swallowed it with greedy, nibbling haste and a muffled duck-grunt. 'You're welcome, but don't quack with your mouth full,' she told him glumly.

Across the pond, the clarion, derisive *Aaack . . . ack . . . ack* of rallying ducks rang out, and two more approached in a purposeful glide, their wakes silver lines drawn across the olive-brown water. Jolian tossed them both pieces, then scowled as the larger bird surged ahead of his mate to gobble up both.

'Pig!' She skimmed a full slice at the slower female, who made a valiant attempt to down it whole and nearly strangled. 'Oops!' Jolian was suddenly very popular and very busy as she dispensed bread and comments to a converging, gabbling mob of ducks. 'Do that *once* more, you bully, and you're on my blacklist!'

'The runt hasn't gotten a bite yet,' The gruff, boy's voice beside her was carefully offhand.

Jolian blinked, then concealed her start with a careful toss. 'I know. He may be little but he's slow . . . You *turkey!*' she gasped as, head low and menacing, a black and white duck churned after the runt.

She turned to the boy and jumped—'*Wo!*'—as her eyes met a funhouse version of her own face reflected in an enormous pair of mirror sunglasses. She watched her eyes widen and her mouth drop.

The impish grin below the glasses turned into a delighted laugh at the look on her face. He pulled the Red Sox cap even lower over his forehead and leered up at her. 'Wanna banana, lady?'

'I don't believe you!' she laughed, shaking her head. 'No one will ever recognise you!' The M.I.T. sweatshirt—three sizes too large—and a scruffy pair of red plaid pants completed his disguise. He was a long way from the clean-cut preppie of Fletch's poster.

'That's the whole idea,' Jem agreed smugly. 'Keep 'em so busy staring at the outfit, they'll never even notice my face.' He glanced towards the water. 'In the meantime, have you ever been mugged by a duck?'

Jolian turned to face a barrage of beady, expectant eyes. Three of the largest ducks were waddling purposefully ashore, their necks craning at the forgotten bag of bread. 'Uh-oh. Here, take some!' She snatched a handful of slices out of the bag and passed him the rest of it. Uttering soft quacks of consternation, the attack squad hustled back to the water as she aimed a piece at their more patient friends. 'I'd just about given up on you,' she told the boy.

Jem bounced a piece off the black and white bruiser and chortled as a smaller duck snatched it from under his beak. 'Oh, I've been here all along,' he said breezily.

'You have?'

'Yup.'

Jolian flashed him a rueful glance. 'Looking for ambushes?'

He looked absurdly young when he was pleased with himself. He nodded coolly.

'Trusting sort, aren't you?'

Jem's smile was apologetic. 'Dad has a way of getting what he wants, especially with women, Jolian ...' He looked back at the ducks. 'And that *is* a lot of money he's offering.'

'Mm-hmm. But I don't sell friends.' She left him to collect the second loaf of bread off her bench, and gave him half of it in silence.

'I'm sorry,' he muttered awkwardly.

'If you were *really* sorry, Jem ...'

The glasses turned towards her uneasily.

'... you'd take off those funhouse mirrors,' she told him gravely. 'I never realised I needed plastic surgery before.'

His grin flashed and he pulled them off. 'You don——' The smile vanished as his voice broke and he tried again. 'You *really* don't,' he said huskily.

She smiled at the compliment and turned back to the ducks. And neither did he. He was going to be as devastating as Fletch some day, but in an entirely different way.

They worked out a system of alternate bread tossing, a game of keep-away which kept the bully birds working for their share of the treats and helped the smaller, slower ducks to snatch an occasional mouthful. Bread gone at last, they retreated. Jolian knew a bakery on Charles Street which served good coffee, and they wandered slowly over the bridge towards the distant gate.

Jem left the glasses off but pulled his baseball cap lower. Jolian slanted a wry glance down at him and slowed her walk to a thoughtful saunter. 'So why did you run away, Jem?' she asked at last.

He scuffed the first golden leaves off the pathway, staring down at them intently. Perhaps she shouldn't have asked yet. 'He didn't need me,' Jem spoke suddenly. He glanced up at her and away, his sensitive mouth pulled into a quivering imitation of Fletch's hard smile. Yanking the bill of his cap even lower, he aimed a vicious kick at a crumpled paper cup on the sidewalk. 'He's tried to be nice, bought me everything he could think of, Jolian, but all the time, I'm just in the way.' They caught up with the cup again and he smashed it on ahead of them. 'He's got his girl-friends in the city. . . his work . . . I just thought maybe he'd be happier if he wasn't stuck with me.'

Jolian gave the cup a gentle toe-tap. 'What makes you think he's not happy?'

'I don't know . . . something . . .the way he looks sometimes . . .' He shrugged.

'He doesn't seem very happy *without* you, Jem.'

'He'll get over it,' the boy said shortly. 'If he knew . . .' He stopped suddenly and shrugged at her questioning glance.

Jolian hooked the cup his way with her instep and frowned. 'So you went to see your mother,' she probed gently.

'Yes,' he nodded, 'for the first time since she left us.' His breath hissed out slowly. 'What . . . happens . . . if you don't like your own mother?'

She shot him a sympathetic look. 'Something dark and furry, with green teeth, pulls you shrieking down the nearest sewer.'

Jem's surprised laughter rang out and he dribbled the cup back to her side of the path. 'She's even more beautiful than I remembered,' he confided. 'She's an actress—in plays, not films.' The laughter was slowly fading from his voice again. 'She spent two weeks trying to act like she cared about me, and finally gave up.'

Jolian collected the cup and dropped it into a trash

barrel as they stepped out on to Beacon Street. Jem put his glasses back on, his smile stiff.

'But your father cares,' she insisted.

The boy shook his head. 'One of them had to take me, Jolian, and of course it would be him, I know that now.' His breath hissed again. 'It doesn't mean he *wanted* me. It's not even fair for *him* to be the one.'

Jolian sighed. He was going to take some convincing. 'Well, I think you're wrong about your father, Jem, but I know how you feel.' She glanced up, noted the gap in the traffic and touched his shoulder. They scampered across the street and fell into step again. 'My parents didn't really want me either.' She straightened her shoulders, surprised herself at the echo of that old pain.

The unrevealing glasses turned her way, showing her a fat-nosed version of her rueful face. 'Were they divorced?' he asked.

She laughed. 'Far from it. They were—are—the most married couple I ever saw in my life! They just didn't want ... didn't *need* ... anybody else. I was an accident.' An accident they'd been careful never to repeat, despite her childhood pleas for a playmate. She stopped automatically to check some art-deco earrings in an antique shop window.

Jem studied her face in the plate glass reflection.

'How do you know that?'

Jolian grinned back at him. 'I got nosy, when I was about your age, and asked my mother.'

He scowled indignantly. 'And she *told* you? They sound like jerks!'

She laughed softly and pulled him away from the window, shaking her head. 'No, they're not. My mother just has a notion that you should always tell the truth. She told me in the nicest way possible.'

'They still sound like jerks.'

She shook her head again. 'It wasn't like that at all, Jem. They made me very welcome. It's just that I ...

always felt like the third wheel. They never quite notice
there's anybody else in the room, when they're together,'
She heaved a deep, silent sigh and that brought back a
winter's evening when she was about Jem's age, the
red-orange light of the flames flickering across her
sketchpad as she sprawled on the hearth, doodling
drowsily, her mother curled in the armchair above her,
asleep with one of her law books open across her lap, one
lock of her dark hair curving across her cheek.

Jolian had looked up to find her father standing in
the doorway, home from one of his frequent business
trips, had watched his slow, single-minded passage
across the room, his eyes fixed on her mother's face.
Just as his fingers touched her mouth, he had sighed,
and it was the soft sound of a man putting down a
heavy load. He hadn't made it home until that instant.

Her mother's lips had turned into his hand before she
woke ... And she, Jolian, had understood at last the
emptiness within herself, had been searching for that
kind of belonging ever since. She wanted to be home to
someone too.

She must have sighed again. 'Jerks,' Jem had
pronounced beside her with all the conviction of youth.

Jolian laughed, shook her head, and let him swing
open the bakery door for her. So who was comforting
whom here? She pulled a deep, appreciative sniff.
'Mmm, you buy the coffee, and I'll buy the cookies.'

Jem shook his head quickly. 'I'll get it, Jolian. What
do you want?'

He chose a table in the corner and sat with his back
to the room. Fletch had raised no fool, she thought,
studying his odd, triangular smile as she bit into a
hermit bar. When he relaxed, his smile wasn't like
Fletch's at all—so why was it familiar? She hadn't seen
a play in New York in years. 'So you still have some
money left, from what your mother gave you?' she
asked idly.

Jem's smile faded. 'Loaned me, you mean. She said if Dad had finally made something of himself, he could afford to pay my way back.' He scowled.

Finally made something . . . 'So your . . . you haven't always had money, then?' she asked, studying her cup guiltily. The urge to pump the boy was well-nigh irresistible.

Jem bit his lip thoughtfully. 'I don't *think* so. I know we had to sell the house and all Dad's tools, when my mother left.'

'His tools?'

'Woodworking tools—table saws and stuff. He used to make things . . . a hobby, I guess.' He took a boy-size bite of his brownie and washed it down with a mouthful of coffee, then flashed a rueful face at his cup. With no one watching, she guessed he would have ordered milk. 'I've still got a rocking horse he made me. It's beautiful, Jolian. I've never seen anything like it anywhere—all these different colours of wood, steam-bent and laminated into all these crazy curves . . .'

'That must have taken a lot of time and love to make,' she pointed out softly.

'Yeah.' The boy sighed, staring down at the table. 'But he hates it . . . keeps telling me I'm grown up now, to stick it in the attic.' His lips trembled. 'It's just in the way . . . like——' He scraped his chair back from the table and stood up. 'You finished?'

'Mmm-hmm.' Jolian pushed aside a half-full cup and followed him outside. He waited for her to choose the direction, so she set a slow pace back towards Beacon Street, where she had left her car. There would be time for a few hours at the studio before her night class. 'So do you have much of that loan left, Jem?' Perhaps when the money ran out, home would look like a better deal.

He laughed shortly. 'I don't have *any* of it left, Jolian. I got mugged the night before I called you that second time.'

'*Mugged!* Did he hurt you?'

Jem shook his head, smiling his father's tough-guy smile. 'They,' he corrected, as if that made it all right somehow. 'Keeping your money in your shoes is sure a waste of time!'

Jolian laughed in spite of herself, then frowned. 'But you . . . what are you . . . doing for money now, Jem?'

He pulled the Red Sox cap further down over his eyes and gave her his gangster leer. 'Livin' by my wits, lady.'

She smiled dutifully, then studied him from the corner of her eye. How many legal jobs could a boy his age and size find in Boston? She didn't like to think of the alternatives. Panhandling, shoplifting, perhaps playing courier for some small-time drug pusher . . .

His answering three-point smile was a trifle smug. The mirrored glasses gave no clues, and they were at her car now. Reluctantly, she fished her keys out of her shoulder bag and leaned back against the car's dented fender, twirling them idly. 'Do me a favour, Jem?'

He frowned, and jammed his hands into the pockets of his ridiculous pants. 'I wish you wouldn't ask, Jolian.'

'Just call him, Jem. Talk with him.'

He shook his head slowly. 'Can't.'

She sighed. 'Well then, here's another favour.' She found her wallet, pulled out a pale grey and black Quicksilver business card. 'That's my home phone number. If you ever want to talk, or eat a home-cooked meal . . .'

'Thanks,' he said gruffly. He bent his head over the card, the bill of his cap hiding his face. After a second he glanced up. 'Cambridge? You're not very——' He stopped.

She waited, smiling. Jem smiled back and shook his head. 'Are you going to tell him you talked with me?'

She frowned thoughtfully, feeling like a tightrope walker. 'Don't you think he'll want to know you're healthy and taking care of yourself?'

Jem shrugged, suddenly glum.

'You know he will.'

'Okay, Jolian, but I can't tell you anything like ...
where I'm staying.'

Her smile was ironic. 'Think I can't keep a secret?'

Standing on the kerb, Jem had perhaps two inches of
advantage over her and he obviously relished them
both. He stared down at her, smiling his cool smile. 'If
you knew, Dad would get it out of you, Jolian. He can
get to people, believe me.'

She did. Oh, did she ever! Well, something told her
that she'd pushed as far as she could today. And it was
best to end on a light note. 'So how's the weather up
there?' she teased.

This cocky grin was his own. '*Super*, lady. just peachy
... keen!'

'As tall as your father is, I expect you'll shoot up
there on your own in another year or so,' she assured
him.

The words wiped Jem's grin away. An expressionless,
mirror-eyed mask gazed back at her. 'Er ... yeah,' he
murmured blankly, '... yeah ...' He tried to smile and
didn't quite make it.

Jolian maintained her teasing face with an effort,
hoping her eyes weren't reflecting her sudden questions.
She reached out and gave the peak of his baseball cap a
gentle tug. 'Don't lose that phone number, Jem.'

'Right ...' he murmured. He was a thousand miles
away. Some place that hurt.

He was still standing on the kerb, motionless, when
she drove off with a wave. Far down the street, in the
rear-view mirror, she thought she saw his hand lift at
last.

CHAPTER SIX

A LAZY man always tries to carry too much. It was one of Katy's favourite sayings, something the nuns had told her in school, and they were right. She really ought to put one down and come back for it. Instead, Jolian stopped on the stairs and took a firmer grip on the two grocery bags that were trying to slither out of her bearhug. And which bag had the eggs in it? No telling. She braced the bags against her hipbones again and trudged upwards—listening for Yaffa's first yowl.

Instead she heard footsteps—someone descending. She edged over to hug the wall, but kept on climbing. With any luck they would pass at the first landing. She looked up as a shadow wheeled across the open space above and then a man stopped short at the top of her flight of stairs.

Her heart stopped with him. Fletch. There was no mistaking that taut, hard-edged shape looming dark against the light from the window beyond.

As he moved again her heart started as well, but with a different rhythm now, as if it were taking the stairs two at a time to meet him. 'Fletch,' she called softly.

'So there you are.' The low voice wasn't quite as smooth as she'd remembered, or perhaps he was just out of breath. He stopped again and waited, let her climb the last few steps to him.

'Hello,' she managed shyly. He was the same. She hadn't imagined a bit of it.

'Hello, yourself.' Casual words. Words that did not match his tight half-smile, nor the intensity of that green-gold gaze that raked her face feature by feature, starting with her eyes and returning to them at last. His

hands reached out to smooth the wind-blown hair back
from her cheeks and lingered to let his thumbs follow
the swoop of her eyebrows. As she smiled, he sighed—a
deep, soft sound. His fingers spread slowly to cup and
lift her face, and he kissed her. 'Hello, silky cat.' He
kissed her again, but the first slow sweetness had
changed to a fast-burning hunger now. His lips were
harder, quicker, his breathing suddenly harsh.

*'Fletch!' Jolian twisted free from his mouth, shivered
as his lips found her throat instead. 'Fletch!' She tried
to laugh. 'Any man with a heart would take these bags
off my hands!'*

*He laughed softly, his hands gliding down to cup her
breasts with the lightest of touches, a touch that sent
hot, crazy tremors shuddering across her body. 'And
any man with a head would know you're at his mercy
right now, with your arms full. How can I resist that?'
His lips found the bare skin at the vee of her open
collar.*

'*Better try* resisting it, friend!' she gasped, the pulse in
her throat hammering against his mouth. 'You're about
to have one dozen eggs, a pound of . . . *ham* . . . and . . .
ten cans of-fff . . .' Her voice failed.

His fingertips—slow mountain-climbers—scaled the
peaks of her breasts where they swelled to stand out
against her thin vee-neck sweater, danced tiny victory
dances as they gained the summits. 'Of what?' he
laughed against her throat.

'Of-fff . . .' *What* had she been trying to say? Oh,
'—of cat food dropped on your toes!' she gulped.
'*Fletch!* Cut it *out!*'

'Uh-oh!' The dark head lifted and his hands slid
gently upward to rest on her shoulders. 'That sounds
like the General speaking. I was wondering where she'd
gotten to.' He grinned down at her, his fingers
tightening reflexively.

There is a name for this, Jolian thought dizzily staring

up at him as she tried to catch her breath. *A most dangerous and lovely name.* And if she didn't distract him now, he would start again, she realised as he pulled her forward. She thumped the bags up against his ribs; they made an excellent blockade. 'Fine. If I'm giving the orders, take these.'

'Yes, *ma'am!*' His voice and eyes mocked her, warned her that delay was a feeble military tactic at best. There was still a battle to be joined.

And nothing has changed, she warned herself as she retreated before him up the stairs, *nothing except that now you know how much you want him. You want him, and he wants you. For a while. Play with this match, Jolian, and he's going to scorch your fingertips right up to the elbows. Right up to the heart.*

'Where have you been all day?' Fletch complained at her heels. 'This is the third time I've stopped by.'

'Working.'

'With Frasier?'

'Who else?' she asked lightly, ignoring the edge to that question. 'He *is* my partner, after all.'

'And you two . . . *work* on Saturdays?' His emphasis suggested more interesting ways to pass the time.

But she was not going to rise to that. 'Saturdays, Sundays and Christmas when necessary, Fletch. We spent all day choosing and photographing the designs we'll use to apply for the American Crafts Council Show in June.'

'The crafts fair at Rhinebeck?'

'Yes. It's a juried show. That means we have to prove to a panel of judges that we're good enough to exhibit there.'

'Yes, I know what that means.' he said dryly, stopping behind her as she found her key ring. 'Have you made the cut before?'

A low, throaty moan greeted the click of the key sliding into the lock. 'Yes,' she told him proudly, 'for the last two years. That's where we make a lot of our gallery contacts.' She hesitated, staring down at the key.

'Try turning it, Jolian. That's how they usually work,' Fletch suggested at her ear.

'Yes ...' But she wheeled to face him, feeling suddenly suffocated by the overwhelming size and nearness of him, and the open desire in the eyes that searched her face.

'Don't be afraid, silky.' It was almost a whisper, laughing words to soothe a treed cat.

Jolian tried to smile. He *could* read her like a book. 'But I *am* afraid. I don't want you to come in, Fletch.' Yaffa seconded that from the other side of the door.

One dark brow rose slowly as he studied her. 'Why not? You should know you can trust me.'

Trust him to break her heart? Without a doubt. 'Trust you to keep your hands off me? I don't think so.'

'You can trust me to do whatever you want,' he said smoothly. A nice evasion. His eyes flicked across her breasts and back to her face and he almost—smiled.

'I don't want you to touch me,' she insisted, crossing her arms in spite of herself. She frowned to make the gesture look stern rather than defensive.

His half-smile became whole. 'And I don't believe you.'

'Then I guess this is what they call an impasse,' she said lightly, her nerves jumping. How far could she push this? When Fletch put those bags down, her game would be up. One touch and she was done for. She leaned back against the door, struggling to hide her fear with a look of bored patience.

His breath hissed in exasperation as he shifted the grocery bags. 'Jolian, don't be absurd. I have to talk to you.'

Talk? Ha! 'So phone me.'

His lips twitched. 'I'd rather talk to you ... in the flesh.' *All of it*, his eyes said.

She shivered suddenly, her body responding to the threat and promise in those eyes. 'You can't come in!' she blurted helplessly. 'I'm tired. I'm not in the mood for a wrestling match. Go away!' She shook her hair back, suddenly furious at being cornered this way. Cornered by him, cornered by her own treacherous desires.

'Wrestling wasn't exactly what I had in mind,' Fletch murmured whimsically. Those green-gold eyes were laughing at her.

She hissed the words at him one by one. 'You can *not* . . . come . . . in!' The realisation that she would lose this confrontation made her all the angrier. She would lose if he stayed, lose if he turned and left her now.

Fletch was frowning now, staring down at her thoughtfully. 'You *really* don't want me to make love to you?' he asked finally, one eyebrow lifting.

His scepticism almost made her laugh. What a healthy ego! He must be good . . . He *was* good. As she remembered his touch, her amusement vanished and she shook her head firmly. *Trouble, Jolian, he is TROUBLE. Be smart for once in your life!* She shook her head again.

Fletch let his breath out slowly—male patience tried beyond all rational limits. 'All *right*,' he said sarcastically, 'we'll call a truce. I promise I won't touch you tonight. How's that?'

'That's not good enough!' Out of her life would be better. Or wiser, if not better. There was no use loving what she couldn't keep.

'That's all I'm offering, lady, and you've got ten seconds to take it or leave it!'

And if she left it? Narrow-eyed, she measured him across the shopping bags, wondering if she could work a better deal than that, a long-term detente.

'Seven . . . eight . . .' Chanting softly, Fletch stooped to set the bags down, his eyebrows at a dangerous angle. 'Nine . . .'

'*Taken!* I take it!' Her words came out with a squeak. Infuriating.

'Wise, lady,' he murmured, eyes glinting, 'wise.'

It took an effort of will to turn her back on him and open the door, an effort to keep her shoulders from shuddering with his eyes boring into her back. Yaffa thumped on to her neck as she passed the counter, wobbled, then caught her balance with lashing tail. Fletch dropped the bags on the table and turned back to the door. 'Where are you——' Jolian bit the question off and reached up to steady her passenger.

Fletch stopped and looked back at her. 'I've something in the car for you.' He pulled her key ring from the lock, stood staring down at it, then looked up with his tough smile. 'So here's your chance to lock me out.' The keys sailed in a clean arc across the kitchen.

Jolian caught them absently, her eyes on his face. For a second, he looked almost vulnerable. Could that smile, that joke hide a touch of uncertainty? 'I won't be doing that,' she told him softly, and his smile faded. Their eyes held for a moment, then he was gone.

No, might as well admit it. She would not lock him out. Could not. Fletch was inside her gates already. It would be about as useful as locking the barn door with the horse thief still inside. Too late, God help her, too late. And speaking of horse thieves, where was he? Jolian had time to feed the cat; brush her hair; choose a soft, long, flowered skirt and a softer blouse; decide that this was too fancy and then put them on anyway, and still he didn't show. Unpredictable, beastly man! She settled at last on the sofa with a glass of Chablis and the newspaper, her ears tuned to the stairwell.

But when the knock came at last, she jumped all the same. He had a thief's light step. 'Who is it?' she teased the door.

'Me.'

Preparation for Fletch's impact didn't really help

much. There was still that little jolt, that catch in the
breathing when she opened the door and their eyes met.
'Hello, you.' The jolt gave way to enveloping warmth as
his eyes flicked over her and widened for an instant
in obvious approval. 'Thought you'd gone back to
Chicago.'

'I walked to the river to cool down.' The faint smile
mocked himself, but the eyes on her face were serious.
'I've been arguing all week, Jolian, and I've had
enough. Let's have a real truce tonight, shall we?' He
moved past her to set a large box on the table, then
accepted one of the long-stemmed glasses she held out.

'Peace,' she agreed, lifting her glass towards him.

'Peace.' The crystal connected with a silvery, magic
cry in the twilight of the room. Their eyes connected as
well. Jolian retreated first, snapped on a lamp, then
curled down on the rug near the sofa.

'For you, lady.' Fletch set the package beside her and
settled back on the couch, his dark eyes expectant.

Jolian studied the box thoughtfully. She shouldn't
take it, whatever it was. It would just be one more link in
the chain he was forging for her, a chain that had a
terrifying heft and length already. She shouldn't open it
at all. She flicked a wary glance up at him. 'Is it Ralph?'
she teased.

Fletch laughed. 'Don't think I didn't consider it! No,
I spent all Sunday night kicking him off my feet, and
that was the last straw. Ralph is running up a bill I
don't want to think about in the poshest hotel in
Chicago.'

So he'd slept at home one night, anyway. But then
who was to say who else had shared his bed besides
Ralph? Catty thought. She turned back to the box,
frowning.

'It's not the . . . sort of thing I usually give, but
somehow I thought . . .' Fletch's voice trailed away
again.

Jolian kept her eyes on the box, pain padding across her heart on little cat feet. *Usually gave.* To women, of course. Yes, of course that was his style. If you won't—can't?—give your heart, give a gift instead. Lots of gifts. Big gifts. Fletch would be generous, no doubt about it. Suddenly, she had to see what price he had set upon her head. The ripping of the cardboard made a sound to match her mood exactly.

Her fingers felt the smoothness of the shape before she could see beneath the packing chips. Eyes widening, she gripped it carefully and heaved it out of the box, then laughed softly and glanced up at him. His gaze was unblinking, carefully blank.

She turned back to the sculpture. It was an upright, deceptively simple form—simple as an unknown shell is simple, one subtle curve flowing into the next. The wood it was shaped from was a mahogany so dark red as to look almost black in the lamplight. '*Mmm...*' Following the silkiness of the hand-rubbed finish, her fingers encountered a crack. No ... a vertical seam. Startled, she looked up at Fletch again.

One corner of his mouth lifted. 'Go on.'

Gently she pulled, and the shape pivoted on invisible hinges, opened into two halves to reveal an interior of pale golden wood. *'Oh!'*

Fletch laughed softly at her delight. 'Keep going.'

In one half of the shape, thin seams followed the darker grain of the wood. There were polished hollows inviting a fingertip. She tugged gently and a slice of wood pivoted towards her. It was a drawer, or tray rather, lined in red cedar. And this was a jewellery box—a box like no other. 'Fletch, I love it!'

'Good,' he said simply.

But what did its giving mean to *him*? Was it just a gift, or more than that? It would be so foolish to hope ... She bent to sniff the aromatic cedar scent and to hide her face for a moment. 'I love it.'

'You're not done yet,' he told her.

With his eyes on her face, she explored the rest of the box. There were three more trays below the first one, each big enough to hold a necklace. The opposite side split again to reveal a new dark wood inside the light. More parts unfolded, a bevelled mirror framed in ebony rose out of a slot to stand above the earring drawers. 'You've thought of everything!' she exulted, looking up at him.

His grin vanished, and suddenly his eyes were wary. 'How ...' He stopped and took a careful sip of wine and she watched his lips curve in that hiding smile of his.

'Yes, you,' she insisted softly. 'You made this.'

'Jem told you?' he asked finally.

'Mmm. He told me about his rocking horse. But he thought this was just a hobby. I know better. Where did you study?'

'S.A.C.' He collected her wine glass and retreated towards the kitchen.

Go to Harvard for a degree in law, M.I.T. for engineering, the School for American Cratfsmen in Rochester for an education in furniture design. She took the refill he handed her with troubled eyes. 'So what in heaven's name are you doing, Fletch, selling unfinished furniture when you can do work like this?'

'*Could,*' he muttered, staring down at the box at his feet as if he might kick it. 'This was the last piece I made, eight years ago ... I'm making a damn good living, my little puritan, that's what I'm doing.'

And hating every minute of it. 'You couldn't make a living doing this?'

'Given ten years to build up a reputation and a clientele with a taste for the finer things in life—and bank accounts to match—yes, I could have. It's not like turning a profit on a fifty-dollar pair of earrings, Jolian.' He slouched down on the couch. 'Woodwork is

slower. Much slower ... The price I'd have to put on
this piece to get my labour back puts it out of the reach
of ninety-nine out of every hundred people that might
want it.'

'And you weren't given the time to find that
hundredth person with the purse to match a taste for
real craftsmanship?' she asked quietly, studying his
masklike face. With one hand, she stroked the glossy
side of his box as she might have touched Yaffa.

'No.' And no intruders wanted.

But she wasn't going to be shut out that easily. Not
now. Not with this piece of his heart in her hands. 'Liz,'
she stated softly. That had to be the reason.

Fletch's eyes switched back from the middle distance
to focus on her face below him. A corner of his mouth
twitched, then slowly lifted. 'Do you know what
curiosity did to the cat, silky?'

'I've three or four lives left,' she counterd with a
smile, ignoring the warning. 'It was Liz, wasn't it?'

He slouched slowly back against the cushions and
shut his eyes, frowning as if his head hurt. She waited.
'Yes,' he muttered finally. Eyes still closed, he finished
his wine, but her silence seemed to annoy him. He
flicked the glass with a restless finger, filling that silence
with its crystalline voice. Still she kept silent, her eyes
on his shuttered face. His lips twisted in a smile of
defeat and he nodded. 'Liz,' he murmured wryly. 'She'd
been in the theatre since she was fifteen, Jolian, most of
that in roadshows. She was sick of it when I met her.
She wanted out, and she wanted out in style.' His
breath hissed, a sigh disguised as anger.

'Style might be asking a lot of a young artist,' Jolian
observed softly.

Still shut off from her, his smile flicked for an instant,
then vanished—a recognition of her partisanship, and a
rejection of it. 'I'm afraid it was more than *I* could
provide, anyway, fresh out of college. And most of

what I earned in those first few years had to go right
back into the workshop for tools, Jolian.' Frowning, he
lifted the empty glass to his lips, then lowered it again
quickly.

Jolian leaned forward to catch his hand, steadied it as
she poured most of her wine into his glass. Looking up,
she looked into his eyes—too close, too warm.
Retreating before the heat of that blaze, she sat back on
her heels. 'And Jem must have come along pretty soon
after your marriage,' she guessed hastily.

The flame flickered out of Fletch's eyes, leaving them
cold and distant. 'Yes. Yes, indeed he did.' His smile
was almost savage. Slowly it softened at some memory,
then it hardened again. 'Young Jem presented himself,
post haste.' His eyes came back to her and the present
and now his words were brisk, a curt summing up.
'Given another four years, I could have provided some
style, but the lady didn't care to wait. She'd gone back
to acting locally after the third year. She was missing
the bright lights, all the——' a nerve fluttered beneath
his eye for a second, 'all the *attention* by then. I wasn't
proving to be quite the investment she'd hoped, so . . .'
He shrugged and finished the wine in one gulp,
smacked the glass down on the side table with
deliberate finality. The look he gave her clearly warned
her to pry no further.

'But . . .' But she must. Jolian frowned, looked down
at his box for courage and then up at him again. 'But
why didn't you keep on after she left, Fletch?'

He stared at her almost bitterly. 'Because the lady
wanted *money*, love, as most of 'em do, sooner or later!
She needed cash to storm Broadway. So we traded.'

'Traded?'

'Liz took the proceeds from sale of the house, the
studio, the tools. She took the car. In return, I got
uncontested, total custody of Jem, who she'd never
wanted anyway. And then she took the last laugh.' His

brows came down in a thunderous line at the question in her eyes. He snatched the wine glass out of her hand and stalked towards the refrigerator.

He was about three questions from lift-off, Jolian calculated swiftly. But she was still getting answers, and that was worth almost any explosion. 'And then?' she asked deliberately, taking her glass from him.

As he towered above her, his look was near murderous. As she met and held it, chin up, it wavered, softened finally to incredulous, rueful amusement. He grinned slowly, crookedly, shaking his head. 'If I were you, I'd re-tally those lives, silky cat. I bet you've got less than three left!'

'And then?' she coaxed, widening her eyes at him teasingly.

Fletch shook his head in mocking defeat and sat down. 'And then I went out and got a job, and then a better job as a buyer for a furniture store. I saw the gap in the market, borrowed money from my——' he frowned, calculating, 'my second stepfather, opened a store, did well, opened another store, made my first million four years ago, etc, etc, etc, and what else would you like to know, love—the middle name of my maternal grandfather, or my history marks in fifth grade?' He eyed her with wary exasperation.

Yes, some day she would like to know those things as well. She would give Yaffa, Quicksilver and a year off her life to know every last detail that made Fletch what he was, but right now ... 'I have just two last questions,' she stated with soft defiance.

Fletch threw back his head and laughed. 'I asked for that, God help me, I asked!' he told the ceiling. He looked down mockingly. 'Ask away, but you will pay for this, sweet lady, you will pay.' The look in his eyes told her how.

Jolian couldn't sustain that look. She looked down at his box, waiting for her cheeks to cool, listening to his

soft laugh above her. Yes, she would pay, one way, if
not the other. But not tonight. He had promised. She
looked up again. 'How many stepfathers have you
had?' she asked gently.

Fletch's amusement might never have been. He stared
down at her, his face a frozen blank. He took a deep
breath. 'Four, last time I counted. But that's just a
running total—she's between men right now.' His
breath hissed and he took another drink.

It hurt her almost as much as it did him. She
clenched her teeth against the inner vision of a quiet,
dark boy watching the procession of lovers, the
marriages failing and falling, and the final failure—his
own marriage. Had Fletch ever seen a love go *right*?
Even his love for Jem was failing them both somehow.

'And your last question?' he asked, his jaw tight.

She should not have asked that last one first. She'd
lost all his good will again. She opened her mouth, shut
it nervously, but Fletch was waiting, his brows a jagged
line above the wary eyes. 'Well, now that you've made
your millions, why . . . don't you go back to designing
furniture?'

Fletch let his breath out slowly, shaking his head in
disbelief. He took a deliberate sip of wine, sat turning
the glass and staring at it. Finally he spoke, placing the
words between them with savage precision. 'When you
are thirty-seven, my kitten, you may find that the world
isn't all shiny and new when you wake up each
morning. I've made two starts in life. I'm supposed to
quit a successful career and start again?'

'The third time's the charm,' she said softly.

Laughing bitterly, Fletch shook his head, put his glass
down and reached for her. His fingers combed into her
hair and tightened as he tilted her head back with rough
ease. 'You are the charm,' he growled huskily, his face just
above her. 'And I didn't come here tonight to tell you my
life story, I came here to make love to you.'

If only there were some way to take his love, not be harmed by it! Jolian shuddered in his hands, more with her own desire than his own. 'This last half hour, I'd have said you were closer to making war on me than love,' she joked, hoping for a smile.

But the smile he gave her was hardly a kind one. 'And you'd have said right, silky, but they're not the opposites you think—love and war.' His fingers twisted further into her hair and tightened again with a sensual, ruthless pleasure. 'Right now I'd like to love you till you cry for mercy, and I don't think I'd give it, even then,' he whispered, slowly swaying her forward.

Shutting her eyes against the oncoming fire of that green-gold gaze, she saw instead the shadowy battlefield, the clash of bodies, the moans, the overwhelming weight and strength, the final exultant surrender. 'You *promised*!' she cried as his breath warmed her face.

'God*damm*it, Jolian!' The momentum of the embrace was past stopping, but Fletch twisted his head aside, pressing her face into his shoulder instead. 'Do you torture *all* of your men like this, or is it just *me*?' His cheek rubbed across her hair in an angry, frustrated caress as his arms locked around her shoulders.

What other men? There was not another man in the world, not for her! Not answering, she burrowed closer into his solid warmth, glad to be free of his eyes for the moment, dizzy with the scent of his skin, the thunder of his heart against her forehead. 'You promised!' she whispered defiantly, just beginning to realise that he would keep that promise. To be in his arms, and yet to be safe from him. She felt suddenly, wonderfully reckless—the wine going to her head, no doubt. She snuggled under his chin, smiling now.

'You're driving me crazy, woman!' It was half a laugh, half a groan against her hair as he crushed her closer. 'Do you want me to keep that promise or don't you? What the hell *do* you want?'

You, you, you stupid man! Jolian pushed against his chest and his arms loosened, let her lean back in his hold to laugh up at him. Surely he could read that answer in her eyes?

But Fletch stared down at her, dark brows slanting in incredulous, bewildered amusement. 'Do you really want me to keep that promise?'

'Oh, *yes!*' she grinned saucily.

'Oh, *really?*' His half-smile lifted. He let her go, leaned back, resting his arms along the top of the sofa, his eyes mocking her, but the deep, shaking breath he took belied the coolness of that level gaze.

'Yes, really,' she whispered, her hands reaching slowly up to his face. The feel of his skin—warm roughness over hard muscle, harder bone—almost made her shiver as her fingers spread delicately to frame his face.

'Then what the hell's all *this?*' he breathed as she swayed towards him.

'*You* promised not to touch *me. I* made no promises!' she taunted, leaning to kiss the tip of his nose.

But his head shifted in her hands and their lips met instead. Jolian felt Fletch smile with that victory as their lips touched, lifted a breath apart, then moved together again in a slow, circling dance that brought the tears to her eyes. As his breath quickened and she felt his arms start to reach for her, she leaned back. 'Thank-you-for-the-box. I-love-it!' she sang out, bouncing off the couch and spinning away before he could see her eyes.

Yaffa crouched on the carpet, her eyes at their wildest. Jolian scooped her up and buried her nose in the creamy fur, ignoring the growling moan, hearing instead Fletch's deep exasperated breathing behind her. She wandered aimlessly across the room, back carefully turned, giving them both time to cool down. And how could she have *done* that? She'd never be able to look

him in the eye now! *Fool, idiot, impulsive dimwit!* Yaffa
had more brains.

'You're not quite done yet,' Fletch spoke behind her
at last.

What? He expected an encore? Her chin lifted
dangerously.

'With the box,' he clarified, beginning to sound
almost amused.

'Oh?' Yaffa flowed out of her hold, landed on the
carpet on silent feet, her tail tip jerking with irritation.
Jolian took a deep breath. She shouldn't go near him
again.

'No. You missed the secret drawer.'

'You're lying, Fletcher McKay,' she told the far wall.
It was a trap to lure her back. As if she needed it!
Fletch was lure and trap enough.

'I am not. Come and see.'

Fletch was crouching beside the box, his eyes fixed on
a smooth area of wood below the earring drawers. He
didn't look up as she came to hover behind him. 'Pull
this drawer out and reach in behind it, Jolian. You'll
feel the catch.' He pressed with a gentle fingertip and
the bottom section folded out smoothly, showed itself
to be a covered box about two inches square. He smiled
as she knelt beside him. 'The cover slides to the right.'
He made no move to open it.

So she would have to. She whipped a wary glance at
him, met his expectant eyes. His smile widened; he was
confident of this victory. Curiosity kills the cat in the
end, nine times out of nine. She sighed and reached for
the top, slid it aside.

'Oh!' Her fingers curled round the pearl and scooped
it out. It glowed in her hand, much too large, too pink,
too rich to replace the one he had stepped on. He had
paid a fortune for this beauty. 'Fletch, you didn't have
to do this!'

'I pay my debts,' he said quietly.

'You'd paid already—bodyguarding me that night in the Combat Zone.'

Fletch shook his head, smiling. 'I bodyguard for free, silky. But debts I like to pay, and pay promptly.'

Catching the warning note in those words, she looked up to meet his eyes. 'Why is that?'

'That way I can walk, when I'm ready, and not look back,' he said simply, holding her gaze.

She jerked her head away to stare down at the pearl, tossed it up and caught it, tossed it again, watching the silver sphere float and fall through the sheen of her tears. Concentrate on that pearl. Mustn't let it fall. Mustn't spill a tear either. 'Right,' she murmured breathlessly, acknowledging his message. Yes, he would walk some day. When she ceased to amuse him, when Jem was found, Fletch would walk and not look back. It was hardly surprising, given his history, that he'd turned his back on love, wouldn't have it as a gift. So sad for them both, but hardly surprising. She sighed softly.

'Jolian.' Fletch reached out, swept the sheltering curtain of her dark hair aside and draped it behind her ear. She turned her face away. Not yet. In a moment the tears would be gone, but not yet. 'Are you going to hold me to that promise?' he coaxed, tracing the whorls of her small ear with a fingertip.

'Yes.' She dropped the pearl into its hiding place, carefully folded the chest back into its smooth, dark enigmatic shape, a shape as hard and glossy as Fletch himself. 'Yes, I am.'

He sighed and stood up. 'Okay, puritan, *be* that way!' He glanced at his watch. 'I guess we'll use that reservation after all.'

'Reservation?'

'We have a table at the Sky Terrace in an hour. Let's get going.'

She frowned up at him, her hands clasped around the

box in her lap. He'd chosen one of the swankiest restaurants in town, of course. It would be an expensive evening, just one more obligation. Which was no doubt how Fletch wanted her—in his debt. He free to walk; she obliged.

Watching her face, his brows came down slowly. He leaned over, caught her arms and lifted her to her feet, shook her gently. 'What the hell happened to that peace we said we'd have tonight? Can't we agree on *anything*?' He rocked her again, slowly, as if he liked to watch her sway. 'Please?'

He was tired. She could see it now in the tightness of his face, lurking behind the alertness in those dark eyes. Must be exhausting to always have to be in control, to be tough. And her teasing hadn't helped. He didn't need a night on the town, he ought to have an early night in bed, a back-rub, be made to sleep till noon for once in his life. If he were hers, she'd see to that. 'What have you been arguing about all week?' she asked, remembering his earlier remark.

Fletch half-smiled at her change of subject. 'Get your coat and I'll tell you.' ·

'Okay.' So simple to say yes. And it was shocking how much pleasure his satisfied smile gave her as he let her go. Terrifying to realise that she'd not change this evening with him for all the pearls in Boston, no matter what followed.

Outside, the windy afternoon had settled into a crisp, clear night—cool for early October. The leaves still clinging to the trees whispered stubbornly as he handed her into the car. In the headlights, fallen maple leaves skittered across the road like mice on night escapades. Fletch found her hand, his fingers warm and unyielding when she tried to pull back. 'Don't thwart me, woman.'

She laughed and gave up. 'You've been thwarted all week?'

'Mm-hmm.' The car swung out on to the parkway, a

river of headlights following the dark river down towards the sea and the glow of downtown. 'I've been out in California most of the week, trying to put this deal back together.'

'It's coming apart?'

'Looks like it. I've been negotiating to buy a string of import stores out there. You know the type—rice mats and baskets from China, crystal from Finland, tablecloths and pottery from Mexico—basically cheap, pretty household items from all over the world.'

'To go with your cheap, ugly furniture?' she teased.

He took it without offence. 'Exactly. It's a perfect combination.' His low voice was utterly confident, and devoid of all enthusiasm—the businessman, not the artist, speaking. He noted the fork in the road ahead and flicked a glance her way, eyebrow lifting.

'Stay left,' she advised, suddenly depressed. Fletch was right, it sounded like an excellent deal. He would make some more millions, show Liz once again what an investment she had rejected. He would have even less time for Jem, less time for himself, and lots more money he didn't need. Unless the deal fell through, she remembered suddenly. 'So what's the problem?'

Fletch frowned, and changed lanes to let the car behind him roar past. 'It's the young hot-shot who owns the stores. He'd gotten himself over-extended last year, starved for cash. That's when he thought about selling. But now he's come up with some new financing, through relatives out there, and he's decided he wants to buy *me* out.' He sounded almost indignant. 'We've been waltzing round and round all week, getting nowhere.'

'Oh, Fletch!' Jolian slid around on the seat to face him. 'Sell to him. That's perfect!'

'And do what with myself?' He was annoyed, as well as surprised.

'Design furniture,' she said promptly. 'Raise your son. Drop out of the rat race.'

'Damn it, Jolian, I'm doing my best to raise my son, if he'd give me half a chance!'

'Give him half your time and perhaps he would,' she shot back.

'He's got to eat as well,' Fletch growled. He flicked an impatient glance across the river basin as they crossed the Longfellow bridge. Ahead of them, the lights of Beacon Hill formed a glittering foothill for the man-made heights beyond. 'Where do we go now?' He followed her directions, scowling now as he tailed the traffic towards the water front.

She ought to back off. It was not her business after all, but . . . 'Whatever Jem's worried about, Fletch, it's not money.'

He gave a tight, quick shrug as if he could shrug her words away. 'Somebody sure better worry about it . . . Besides, what makes you think I don't *like* racing rats?' He glanced her way, his jaw squared, brows at an ominous angle.

How do you tell a man he looks unhappy? Jolian studied his tight profile, the hands clenched on the steering wheel. 'I . . . just thought . . . You don't really seem to enj——'

Fletch jammed on the brakes as the car ahead stopped short for a yellow traffic light. '*Son* of a ——' He bit it off and shot her a vicious look. 'Well, you thought wrong! I'm having the time of my life!' he snarled.

The contrast between words and tone was too much. She let out a yelp of delight and fell back against her door, giggling. As he shot her another seething look, she sucked in her breath, her eyes widening with the effort to hold it, then exploded again.

'Which way?' he asked her sullenly.

Unable to speak she pointed.

'It's just been a tough week,' he growled finally.

Another giggle escaped her. Jolian pulled a shaking breath and watched his profile.

Slowly his face relaxed. His lips quirked, hardened, then lifted again in spite of his efforts. Fletch shook his head slowly. 'Why do I put up with this?' he marvelled. 'You're not my usual sort at all.'

That cured the giggles. 'What's your usual sort like?' she asked casually.

His smile grew, as if with some memory. 'Not half as argumentative. Twice as ... agreeable.' He flung her a meaning look.

'Perhaps you put up with me because I'm your only connection with Jem right now.' She voiced the fear lightly.

Fletch laughed. 'Perhaps that's it.'

He was in a better mood than she as they walked the bricked plaza and parks along the waterfront. He kept her by his side, one arm draped lightly around her shoulders. The promise not to touch was a relative protection at best, but she was past protecting, touched already. As they walked, she studied their paired feet with glum eyes. Fletch leaned down to inspect her face once, his eyebrow lifting in question, but she smiled for him and looked away. It was not *his* problem, after all. *Snap out of it, Jolian, snap out.*

The table Fletch had got for them at the Terrace— and she didn't care to know how—did much to cheer her. 'Glad I'm not scared of heights!' she breathed as he held a chair for her. Just beyond the plate glass wall beside their table, Boston Harbour stretched away, a world of black velvet and jewels—diamonds and topaz for windows and street lights, rubies changing to emeralds as the traffic lights changed, sapphires to the west on the runways of Logan Airport. Humming a wordless note of delight as a jet touched down, she turned to see if he'd seen it, but his eyes were on her, not the view. Her lashes dropped before that look and she was suddenly glad they were in a public place. Fletch looked in a mood to break promises.

She started from her thoughts as his finger brushed

her bottom lip. 'Glad you like it,' he said huskily. 'We turned the lights on just for you.'

Smiling against his fingertip, Jolian turned back to the window as the waiter arrived and Fletch ordered the drinks. A tug was steaming out of the harbour, pushing a froth of white lace before it across the velvet. She watched it and tried not to think. Feeling was so nice, why spoil it with thoughts?

A warm, slow finger traced the back of her hand as it lay on the table, drawing her attention back to him again. 'So tell me about Jem, now,' Fletch said quietly.

And so. Back to business. Jolian sighed and gathered her thoughts. Feathering along the inside of her wrist now, his fingers did nothing to help their organisation— nor her breathing, for that matter. 'Well . . . I saw him on Wednesday . . .'

The fingers stopped. 'You *saw* him!' he hissed, eyes widening.

'Yes, I . . .' she swallowed suddenly at the look on his face. 'Why——'

'You *saw* him and you didn't hang on to him?' Shock was falling rapidly before incredulous rage, and Jolian was suddenly thankful for the glass between them and the drop off. Fletch looked as if he could cheerfully toss her over the edge at the moment. Her wrist hurt, and she glanced down to find his fingers clamped around it.

'You——' He bit it off as the drinks arrived, but he made no move to release her. She glanced after the discreetly retreating waiter with wistful eyes and then back to Fletch. So much for peace.

'Yes, I let him go, Fletch! What was I supposed to do, take my butterfly net along?'

'You could have hung on to him! Yelled for a cop. It's illegal to be a runaway.'

'Look, maybe *you* take the gorilla approach.' She looked down at her wrist pointedly. 'I don't. He's nearly as big as I am, for starters.'

'You could have——' He stopped, startled. 'But you're—how tall—five foot seven?'

'Five-five,' she corrected.

'He was five feet even in early July,' he muttered, frowning.

'He's grown, Fletch,' she told him gently. 'I bet he's five-two by now at least.' And he'd not been there to see it. She watched the realisation, the loss grow in his face, as his fingers loosened on her wrist. 'Oh, Fletch, I'm sorry!' She reached for his fingers with her other hand, but he snatched them away.

The masking smile was back in place now, a bitter smile. It did nothing to hide the pain in his eyes. 'So am I. Here my detective pounds his flat feet flatter all week and doesn't see one sign of him, and you have him in your hand and let him go!'

'Fletch, force isn't going to help this. Jem has got to decide that he *wants* to come back. That he's *wanted*.'

'Quite the expert, aren't you, lady? I thought you were a jewellery maker,' he jeered.

'Designer,' she corrected edgily. 'But I've worked at the Hotline for five years now, Fletch. I know what I'm talking about. Teenagers are the world's contrariest creatures. You push one way, and he'll jump the other, I guarantee. Force is *not* the answer.' She looked up gratefully as the waiter arrived to take their order.

When he left again, Fletch leaned back in his chair, studying her over his glass, his eyes narrowed. He was making an effort to stay calm, obviously. She smiled for him, pleading for understanding. He scowled and took another drink his eyes never leaving her face. 'Why *do* you work there, silky? Were you ever a runaway?'

She laughed, surprised, and shook her head. 'My parents gave me all the independence I wanted and then some, Fletch! I had no need to be.'

'Why, then?'

She shook her head again. 'Not a nice story. Some other time, Fletch.' She took a quick drink.

The green-gold eyes searched her face. 'Let's have it.' It was an order, not a request.

Jolian sighed, turned to find the tug again. It was long gone. Long gone ... 'In college, Fletch, my room-mate had a kid sister.' She smiled slowly, remembering. 'If I could have had a younger sister, and could have chosen, I'd have picked Jane. She was about five years smarter than she was old ... funny ... just a doll.' She stared down at her drink. Dark, wavering eyes stared back at her—reflections off the liquor's black mirror. She swirled the glass quickly and they whirled away.

'And?' Fletch asked softly.

'And her parents were nice people, but overly protective. They didn't trust her as they could have ... There was some blow-up just before Christmas—Jane stayed out too late. They grounded her, and the next morning she was gone.' She sighed.

'And?'

'And she was *gone*,' she murmured, shrugging helplessly. 'There was one possible sighting in a truck stop between here and Philadelphia. She was hitching up to see us—I'm sure of it. And then ... that was all.'

'*Ever?*' Fletcher's voice was incredulous. As he searched her face, she could see the strain around his mouth. The nerve under his eye ticked for an instant, then stilled.

She should have found some way not to tell him this. Not tonight, as tired and worried as he was. But it was too late now. Jolian hurried to finish the story. 'Ever,' she agreed gently. 'Sandy, my room-mate, heard about the Hotline and wanted to volunteer, just on the long shot that Jane might call some time. But they wouldn't take her. The rules say no relatives of present runaways may work there—they're too involved. Their hearts break each time they pick up the phone and it's not for them.'

'So you volunteered.'

She nodded. 'Almost as a spy, at first. And then I got
hooked, as I saw what good it did. So I stayed on, years
after we gave up on . . .' She stopped, shrugged, and
tried to smile.

Fletch was staring right through her, eyes dark, his
face frozen, long fingers wrapped around his drink. She
saw the knuckles whiten and reached for them with both
hands. He would break the glass that way. *Fletch,
that's not going to happen with Jem!* She stroked his
hands, watching his eyes slowly re-focus on her face.
'That's . . . not . . . going . . . to . . . happen,' she
soothed, her eyes holding his now. 'Jem's not going to
vanish. He's here in town, he's healthy, he's not sleeping
on the street . . .' She felt his hands relax and let go of
him.

He let his breath out slowly, a long controlled sigh, as
he studied her face. His own was oddly vulnerable for
the moment, strangely mobile, as if the mask had
slipped and too many emotions were fighting to come
through at once. Anger still tensed the eyebrows, pain
and a kind of questioning shadowed his eyes, his half-
smile wavered—almost tender, then tough, almost
tender again. His gaze dropped abruptly and he took a
quick drink. When he looked up again, it was all gone.
He looked years older, years tougher, in control. 'What
makes you think he's not sleeping on the street, Jolian?'

So much for emotions. Back to fact-finding, she
thought wryly. 'He's much too clean . . . He's not
sleeping in doorways, I'm sure of it. Are you sure he
doesn't have a friend here in town, Fletch? Someone he
could stay with? Maybe someone who moved from
Chicago recently?'

He shook his head impatiently. 'I've checked all that.
I even had his tent-mates from the computer camp
tracked down. They were all Midwesterners.'

'*Computer* camp?' she laughed. 'You mean that's

what you packed him off to this summer, Fletch? One of those computer-literacy camps for earnest young eggheads?' She shook her head and laughed again. 'I thought you meant a canoe and campfire kind of camp!'

His brows came down, but one corner of his mouth lifted for an instant. 'It had campfires too,' he defended himself. 'But I guess Jem doesn't like computers any more than you do. I just got his evaluation card in the mail.'

'Not so good, hmm?'

He shook his head, smiling in spite of himself. 'It's not as if he's stupid. You should see the marks he makes in English at school, Jolian. But computers . . .' He shrugged and smiled again.

She laughed and finished her drink. 'Computers and evaluations for summer camp. I'd have run away from you too, Fletch!'

'Would you?' he whispered, leaning forward, his eyes stroking her face as if he were touching her. 'Would you really run away from me, silky?'

She tried to smile and couldn't, then shut her eyes against this attack, her hands clenching around each other in her lap. That he could enter and own her with just a look . . . That she could *think* of giving heart and body and . . . happiness to this man who could give nothing in return . . . Was she so stupid? She should run so far, so fast——

She jumped, then sat still as Fletch's finger touched the bridge of her nose, stroked slowly downward, tracing her profile. 'Silky?' His fingertip paused at her lips as if to stop their trembling. Then it moved slowly sideways, out to the corner of her mouth and back again, seeking her smile. She gave him a blind, crooked one and turned to the window, her lashes blinking desperately. All the jewels were comets now, with lovely, gleaming, smeary tails. From the corner of her

eye, she saw a saucer hover into view, come in for a
landing on the tablecloth—food and diversion at last.
Preparing her own form of guarded smile, she turned
back to Fletch, met those alert eyes below the tilted
eyebrows with a rueful little shrug. Should she run? Oh,
yes. *Would* she run? She didn't know, herself.

Over the meal, he took her back over her meeting
with Jem, extracting every fact, every impression that
she could give him, anything at all that might prove a
clue to his son's whereabouts, activities, mood. It was a
thorough inquisition, far more skilful than the one she
had put him through that afternoon, and by the time he
was done, Fletch had it all. Even the facts she had
meant to keep back.

He paid the bill with a bank card, signing the receipt
without flinching, and turned back to her, his face grim.
'So he was mugged ... And you wonder why I'm
worrying so, why I want him off the streets, Jolian?
What happens the next time, if he doesn't have money
for them? Those types tend to get violent, if you can't
produce.' His fingers drummed on the table nervously.

She nodded, searching for some bright spot. 'But he
did have money on Wednesday, Fletch. He's got a job
of some sort.'

Fletch scowled. 'That's supposed to make me feel
better?' He shook his head slowly. 'If I'd had to say one
thing about Jem, I'd have said he was honest.' He
shrugged, smiled lopsidedly. 'Well, he's surprising me in
all kinds of way this year, so ...' He shook his head
again, angrily, trying to shake off that thought. His eyes
returned to her face with a moody, dark look that took
her in feature by feature, that lingered on her lips,
plunged into her hair like an angry, possessive hand—as
if she were something he owned, needed and didn't
quite like. 'Want to dance?' he asked abruptly, jerking
his chin towards the music in the next room.

Jolian shivered in spite of herself—that almost made

him smile—and shook her head. In his present mood, she would have rather danced with a mugger. She could imagine his arms flexing with tension and frustration, pulling her too close, and closer yet, the hammer of his heart beating against her breasts, the pulse of the music, his quickening breath in her ear, perhaps his lips on her face, his hands ... She shivered again. 'No, thank you.'

'Scaredy-cat!' he taunted softly.

She put on a saucy, defiant smile, her chin up. 'Or perhaps I just don't want to dance with you, Mr McKay!' she teased.

His half smile faded as his eyes darkened, travelled over her in a slow burn of a look. 'I want to dance with *you* tonight, silky ... Horizontally not vertically.' He stood up, towering above her. 'Let's go.'

Her knees might not support her; they felt as melted as the rest of her after that look. She should *not* get up, should *not* go with him, should catch a taxi home. Had she brought enough money?

'Let's *go*, Jolian,' Fletch repeated, one eyebrow lifting.

'You *promised*,' she reminded him desperately, her head thrown back to see his face.

The corners of that hard, beautifully-defined mouth deepened and lifted a little. Something seemed to amuse him. 'So I did.' He touched the hollow of her throat with one finger, traced a warm, slow line up to her lifted chin and chucked it gently. 'So I did. Stop worrying and let's go.'

In the car, Fletch's mood had changed again. He went back to his son. 'And Jem said nothing else about anything Liz might have said, beyond what you've told me already?'

In the flicker of passing lights, Jolian studied his tensed eyebrows, the swell of clenched muscles at the back of his jaw. What was he expecting, that Liz had turned Jem against him somehow? 'No, Fletch, I think I've told you everything.' She frowned thoughtfully, trying to remember.

'And *why* did he say he'd run away?'

'He said you didn't need him,' she repeated obediently.

'Need ...' He mouthed the word carefully, as if he hadn't heard it before, and didn't much like it. '. . . need him ... Dammit, Jolian, I love the kid, want what's best for him, but *need*?' He glanced over his shoulder and changed into the other lane. 'I don't *need* anybody,' he murmured absently. His frown deepened in puzzlement and he shrugged.

She shivered violently, and hugged herself, leaning back against the seat, her widened eyes fixed on the path of the headlights, the pavement rushing forward to meet them.

Fletch reached out, brushed her cheek with his knuckles. 'Cold? I can put the heater on.'

'No, that's okay,' she murmured. She was careful to control the shudder this time, tensing her shoulders to contain it. *I don't need anybody*. No car heater would touch this chill ... no heater would melt the ice in his heart either. *I don't need——*

His hand curled around the back of her neck, fingered the tight muscles there. 'What's the matter, cat?' His fingers rubbed her slowly, the hard, slow gentleness of that touch loosening the tension in spite of her resistance. 'Mmm?'

Jolian closed her eyes and tried to think, but thoughts seemed to melt into sensations, treacherous body. She frowned, thought harder. 'So you don't need anyone, Fletch ...' She arched her neck back against his hand and sighed softly. It felt so good. She frowned again. 'But how do you feel right now? Jem's supporting himself, seems reasonably happy, doesn't really seem to ... *need* you ...' She felt his fingers jerk and turned to look at him, but his face was a mask. 'How do you feel about that, Fletch?'

He scowled at the road suddenly. 'Have I gone past the turn-off?'

'Half a mile more,' she assured him, careful not to smile. She reached up, caught his wrist, pulled his hand around to her cheek and rubbed against it slowly. 'Feels pretty rotten, doesn't it?' she said softly.

His head jerked down in just the slightest, tightest of nods. His arm flexed as if he wanted to pull his hand away. She rubbed her lips slowly across it, her eyes on his profile. 'So how do you think Jem's felt, all these years, not being needed?'

As he yanked his hand free, his mouth twisted in what looked like a smile and was not. His eyes squeezed shut for an instant and then opened all the wider to stare at the road ahead. '*Will you shut——*' the words trembled to a halt and he swallowed. 'Will you *lay off*, lady?' He flashed her a savage look. '*Will* you?'

She nodded rapidly, gave a tentative flip of her hand as her corner came into view. They were moving too fast. Fletch had to step on the brakes to make the turn, tyres squealing. He swore, the words all the more vicious for their quietness. Neither of them spoke again until the car was parked. Fletch leaned back in his seat, stared up at the ceiling, let his breath out in a long, shaking hiss.

Wishing she could touch him, not daring to, Jolian waited. She shivered again, this time with the cold.

The corner of his mouth jerked, breaking the mask for a second. 'You *are* cold.'

'A little.'

Slowly, he sighed again. 'Go inside. I'll be up in a minute.'

She stared at him doubtfully. She hadn't meant to let him back in tonight, but now . . . now she was almost afraid to leave him like this.

'Go.' For all its quietness, it was a command. She went.

Coffee, that was what he needed. Coffee and talk. Talk to break this ice-jam of emotions ... Talk—if he would just *talk*! With cat tiptoeing at her heels with plaintive cries, Jolian put the kettle on to boil, set out the cups and saucers, then stood frowning down at them. She had got close to him tonight, closer than she'd ever been before, so close it had hurt him ... Brandy. Perhaps a glass of brandy on the side, to loosen his tongue?

Yaffa darted across the kitchen and under the table, ears laid back. Jolian heard a step, but his arms wrapped round her waist before she could turn and Fletch buried his face against the back of her neck. She shuddered and leaned back against him, her eyes shut. He warmed her skin with a deep, slow sigh as his arms tightened, making it even harder to breathe. She reached up to cup his cheek with her palm and he turned his lips into it and kissed it. She sighed happily. 'I'll have some coffee for us in a minute, Fletch.'

She felt his laugh. His lips came back to her nape, nuzzled her slowly there as he shook his head. 'Don't want any coffee,' he murmured against her skin.

Fool! She should have expected this. What better way to shut her out, to change the subject, than sex? The best defence was a good offence, after all. Jolian swallowed hard as his fingers spread across her rib cage and began slowly, so slowly, to climb. 'Fletch, we've got to talk. How about some brandy?' she gasped.

He brushed her nape again, moved his lips to the top of her shoulder, bit her gently there. 'I'm drunk on you already, silky cat.' His hands closed lightly, warmly round her breasts, and he laughed softly as she shuddered and arched her back.

'Fletch, you *promised*!' she breathed. 'You said you wouldn't——' Her voice feathered into a shaking gulp for more air as his fingertips teased her taut and throbbing nipples. Squeezing her eyes shut, she arched her neck back against his shoulder. 'Please . . .'

'What time is it?' His voice was a laughing, husky whisper in her ear. 'Mmm?'

'No . . . *ahhhh* . . . idea . . .'

'So open your eyes and see,' he teased. He was stroking both her breasts with his right hand now, the thumb and fingers stretched wide.

Jolian opened her eyes, tried to focus them on the wrist floating before her face. Fascinated, she stared at it. So much more powerful, so much larger than her own, the hair dark and curling around the gold links of the wrist-watch . . .

'What time is it?' Fletch reminded her, rubbing his lips slowly along the side of her face.

'Ten after twelve,' she murmured dizzily, 'why . . . *oh!*' She stiffened with outrage, her eyes widening. '*You*——' His arms loosened and she spun around within his hold. He *was* laughing. '*You*——'

'Promises turn to pumpkins at midnight, Cinderella.' His hands stroked slowly down to her hips, cupped them gently and pulled her up on tiptoe against him. 'It's a new day.'

'You planned this!' she stormed. She caught at his shoulders as he leaned forward, arching her back. 'Fletch!'

'It crossed my mind a few times,' he admitted, laughing down at her, his fingers kneading her hips with a slow, fierce pleasure. 'Helped me to be patient when you were teasing.' His lips found her throat and the sound he made as he kissed her was more growl than groan.

'*Fletch* . . .' She had breath for a whisper, no more. 'Fletch, I told you——'

His mouth caught the words, forced them back into her, showed her a better use for lips and breath. Jolian clung to him blindly, shuddering with desire. She gasped for air as he freed her at last, gasped again as his arms shifted and he swung her off the floor. 'Fletch, I——'

'I know what you told me, silky.' His arms tightened, hugging her closer, and his lips brushed her ear. The room spun or he turned—with her eyes shut, she wasn't sure which. 'But your words say "Don't touch me" and those blue eyes say "Come", and tonight, the eyes have it.'

Fletch was moving so gently, so slowly that she could have been floating. They passed the stove and she could hear the kettle simmering. *The pot will boil dry*, a sane, tiny voice remarked in her brain. *Let it!* cried another as Fletch stopped to kiss her again, *Burn the whole house down!* Her hand twisted into his hair as she opened her mouth to him.

They were falling, now, slowly, so gently, a slow-motion, tumbling free-fall, then landing on clouds, Fletch on top. Her body arched to meet his weight as they sank into the cushions of the sofa. 'Fletch!' she begged.

But he mistook it for protest and rolled off her, pulling her with him so that they lay on their sides, nose touching nose. Inhaling hungrily, as if the air they shared was not enough for them both, they lay still, eyes locked. His hands slid slowly upward to hold her face, his thumbs brushing the tips of her lashes. 'Don't try to deny it,' he whispered fiercely. 'You want me.'

And captive of his hands and his eyes, she shook her head. No, there was no denying this.

Eyes blazing with triumph, Fletch kissed her again, a hot, hungry, driving kiss that left her moaning against his lips, arching herself against him from mouth to knees. 'Then say it!' he growled. 'Say you want me!' His arms wrapped around her waist, crushing the breath from her.

'I want you!' she gasped against his throat. With more air she would have laughed her joy, a joy that was pain, anger and jubilant, rushing blood—the fierce, mad need to hold him closer and still closer. 'I want you for ever, Fletch!'

A slap in the face would have had the same effect. His head jerked back, the green-gold eyes widening, and then he was still, except for his deep, painful breathing. 'We're . . .' He swallowed and tried again. 'We're not . . . talking about for ever, silky, we're talking about tonight.' His faint half-smile was almost pleading as he searched her eyes.

Jolian shook her head against the cushions, her nose brushing his as she did so. 'I love——'

He stopped her words, his fingers rough in their quickness. She kissed them defiantly, her eyes beginning to blaze with tears and rage. The fool! The stupid, stupid, *stupid* fool! And she more fool yet for loving him!

'Don't. Don't spoil it,' he whispered urgently. His fingertip caught the first tear and brushed it away. Another trickled after it. 'Don't cry for the moon, cat, when we've got the whole earth tonight. Don't.'

She shook her head savagely. 'I *want* the moon. I want it all. I love you!'

Fletch shut his eyes, shook his head slowly, frowning as if it hurt. Rolling away from her on to his back, he lay still, taking the deep, careful breaths of a diver about to make the plunge. '*Hell*,' he breathed finally. Slowly, he found a smile, a cool, blind smile that seemed to mock them both. 'Hell.' He took another deep breath and sat up.

'Where are you going?' But she knew already. Half blinded by tears, she could still read the answer in those squared shoulders.

Fletch sighed softly, then turned to look down at her. His hand came up, slowly; as if of its own accord it reached out to smooth her tears away. More fell and his smile was suddenly tender. He wiped her cheeks again. 'If you can't follow the rules, I can't play with you, silky,' he murmured ruefully.

'I'm *not* playing.' She shook her head against his fingers, tried to smile, failed miserably.

'I know it. That's why I've got to go.' His fingers lingered on her cheek and he sighed again. 'Would have been fun . . .'

Fun! She winced, squeezing her eyes shut. 'Go to hell, you coward!' she whispered.

He laughed softly and she felt him bend above her. Warm, gentle lips brushed her eyelids. 'You'll live, silky cat,' he breathed. His mouth found the top of her breast, moved slowly and hungrily there. She arched up against his lips, moaning a wordless plea. 'You'll live, if you can still hiss,' he whispered against her skin. 'I'll be in touch in a few days .... about Jem.' The sofa rebounded as he stood up.

Jolian lay rigid, her face turned away from his eyes. *Don't move. Don't think.*

Soft, slow footsteps . . . the door opening. 'I'm . . . sorry, kitten.' Sound of the door closing, the knob rattling as he checked to see that the lock had caught . . . Light, descending . . . *retreating* footsteps.

She lay still. *Don't move yet. Don't try to think.*

A soft *thump* on the sofa near her feet. Gentle vibration of padding velvet paws; the cool tickle of whiskers against her cheek. 'Oh, God, Yaff!' Blindly, she reached out, hooked an arm around the cat, pressed her mouth into the soft fur. Oh, God.

CHAPTER SEVEN

You can't miss what you've never had. Jolian had never had Fletch's love, not for a minute, so how could she miss him so?

You can't miss what you've never—The phrase had a dogged beat, it became a refrain of muted, stubborn, numbed endurance to match her thoughts and her dragging footsteps as she slogged through that week.

You can't miss what you've—always wanted. *Always. Didn't know exactly what till I saw him, but always . . .*

You can't miss what—What if they *had* made love? What if she'd——? What if he'd——? What if . . .?

You can't miss—him. *Ha. Just Watch me!*

You can't—go on like this . . . *Can you?*

You—fool. *Oh, Fletch, you fool . . .*

'You——' Jolian swallowed hard and leaned back against her kitchen counter, squeezing her eyes shut. She should *not* have answered the phone. 'What do you want, Fletch?' Her voice didn't sound quite right—rather hoarse. She swallowed again.

'That's a stupid question, Jolian. You know what I want.' The long-distance connection was not too good; his low voice had all its bite, but none of its usual smoothness.

'I haven't heard from Jem since you—since I saw you last,' she said quickly. There, her voice was working now, if she could only stop shaking. Got to end this, get back to her numbness. One word and he'd wrecked half a week's worth of forgetting. With her eyes shut, she could see those strange eyes, that tough, tender mouth . . . 'Good——'

'*Wait.*' It was a whipcrack of a word. Her hand stopped automatically. 'That wasn't the question. Not the first one, anyway.' His breath hissed slowly in her ear and her body responded with a slow, convulsive shudder.

Her fingers were hurting. Opening her eyes, Jolian stared down at her bloodless knuckles wrapped around the receiver. *Got* to end this. 'What——'

'Where did you sleep last night?' Fletch's half-whisper rasped across her question. 'And where have you been tonight? It's past eleven, your time, and I've been trying to reach you since——'

The gentle click of the receiver dropping back into its cradle cut him off. So simple, really, just hang up. Shut him out of her life, since he didn't want to come into it. Still shaking, Jolian stared down at the phone. Where *had* she slept last—oh, yes, of course. She hadn't slept; no wonder she was so woozy. She'd taken a night shift at the Hotline for—the ring of the phone sliced across her thoughts, a brutal, demanding sound—for Katy, she thought absently, her eyes fixed on the phone. Katy whose love-life was—she flinched as it rang again—was going too well to leave her time for—'Oh, shut *up!*' she gasped as the phone shrilled again. 'Shut . . . *up!*'

She didn't have to take this! She could cut its damn cord, drown it in the sink—'*Shut up!*'—oh yes . . . She could unplug it. Fingers shaking, she snatched at the cord where it snapped into the wall socket. The demanding, maddening racket failed in mid-ring. '*Ahh . . .*' Jolian slumped down slowly on the linoleum, still clutching the cord, staring up at the phone on the counter, half expecting Fletch's magic could make it ring again.

It stayed silent. Slowly she drew a deep breath. 'And tonight,' she told him softly, 'I taught a class how to set their first stones . . . a bezel setting . . . you should have seen their faces.' Yaffa rubbed against her arm and she stroked her absently, her brimming eyes on the telephone. And now she would not sleep tonight either ... 'Oh, *damn* you!' she whispered.

You can't miss what you've never had—a numbing, dogged refrain. By Friday the worst was over, Jolian told herself. She was numb. Work and more work had started the cure; time would complete it. If Fletch just gave her the time ... stayed out of her life. Well, there were ways she could keep him out. *Would* keep him out.

Right now, she had more immediate problems, Jolian thought grimly, staring out the open window at Yaffa.

She jumped as the phone rang behind her. 'Don't go away!' she warned the cat unnecessarily. Just *let* that be Fletch on the phone, she thought savagely. She'd give him an earful today! 'Hello!' she barked.

'... Hello? ... Jolian?' The boy's voice was hesitant, gruffness masking the shyness of his greeting.

'Jem!' Jolian found herself smiling in spite of herself—an odd sensation. She hadn't smiled all week. 'How are you?'

'Oh, not bad. I was ... just ... wondering how you were?' It was a tentative, hopeful question.

Her smile was rueful this time. So he wanted to talk. If she had half a brain she'd tell the kid she was busy, forget him as she was trying to forget his father.

But then what other link did Fletch have to the boy but her?

None. And whatever *her* needs, Jem still needed a home and a father. And Fletch needed his son ...

Jolian pulled a deep breath. He'd asked a question, hadn't he? Oh—'How am I? At the moment, I have a cat up a tree, Jem—a very tall tree—and I'm trying to balance my cheque book, which isn't balancing. That's how I am—just ... peachy keen!'

He laughed, sounding so much like his father that she flinched. 'I didn't know you had a cat.'

'*Had* is the word,' she assured him, turning to peer

out the window. A pale patch of fur swayed into view as the wind moved the branches. 'One slip and I've got a two-tone pancake, not a cat. She's three stories up, the dimwit!'

'Sounds like you could use McKay's Feline Retrieval Service,' he told her, suddenly at ease. 'Treed cats are my speciality.'

'Do you provide back-up scrape and burial services?' she teased.

'For you, lady—anything. Just tell me how to get there.'

Jolian checked her watch as she hung up the phone. This should prove interesting. Yaffa was still nailed to her tree limb about ten feet above the fire escape, her eyes blue saucers. She let out a low moan, as if too loud a yowl might knock her from her perch. Or maybe her voice was finally failing. 'Hold on,' Jolian advised her kindly, and went back to the kitchen. She had the makings for brownies, if she worked fast.

The brownies were just in the oven when Jolian heard feet clattering up her stairs. She checked her watch. Ten minutes. So her hunch must be right; Jem had to be living in Cambridge. *Elementary, my dear Watson.* Smiling, she opened the door to find not one but two half-out-of-breath boys on her doorstep—Jem and a boy half a head taller. 'McKay's Feline Retrieval Services?' she asked, masking her surprise with a teasing grin as she waved them inside.

'At your service, ma'am.' Jem swept off his baseball cap with a graceful flourish, then tugged his taller, red-faced friend forward. 'Ms. Jolian Michaels, this is my intrepid assistant, Kyle Taylor.'

'Hello, Kyle.'

Apparently tongue-tied, the boy nodded jerkily and backed up a step, jamming his hands into his pockets. 'Hi,' he managed finally, directing it more to his tennis shoes than her face.

'Where's the subject?' Jem wanted to know, his voice brisk.

'Right out here,' she told him, leading the way to the open window. 'I let her out on the fire escape for some sunshine, and next thing I knew . . .'

While Jem sized up the situation with all the authority of a professional, Jolian studied his friend from the corner of her eye. She would guess he was sixteen, perhaps a very immature seventeen. He was almost as fair as Jem, but there the similarities ended. Where Jem was still gracefully compact, Kyle was a shambling young crane. Where Jem seemed to be basically outgoing, his friend was painfully shy, and while Jem showed all indications of being outrageously handsome some day, this boy would have a nice, birdy face. He shot her a glance and looked away quickly, but now she had one more similarity for her list. He was as bright as Jem—perhaps not articulate, but bright. Those pale grey eyes were uneasy, but very, very wide awake.

Jem scrambled out the window.

'Jem, what are you going to——' It suddenly occurred to Jolian that a treed cat was the least of her worries. If Jem broke his neck, no doubt Fletch would wring hers for her as well.

Jem leaned back into the room. Behind the façade of breezy command, his eyes gleamed with a fierce, almost manic joy. 'Kyle, come gimme a hand!'

The older boy groaned and flashed her a wry glance. He climbed out with a careful bending and sorting of long limbs that still resulted in a tangle as Jem pulled him through the window.

Heart in her mouth, Jolian leaned after them. *Two* boys with broken necks—marvellous! Stepping into Kyle's clasped hands and then up to the fire escape railing, Jem hoisted himself on to the roof and disappeared from view. 'Jem, be careful!' she pleaded. Why had she ever started this?

'Piece of cake, lady,' he sang out from above. 'Come on out and get your baby!'

And just how much weight was this fire escape meant to hold? Jolian stepped up and swung through the window. Catching the bony paw that Kyle offered her, she stood up beside him on the iron grating. Piece of cake, indeed! Pie in the sky was more like it. *Just don't look down.*

On the slope of the roof, Jem was grappling with the lower twigs of the large branch that waved above him. She gasped as he jumped for the branch itself and missed. *'Jem!'*

Ignoring her, Jem jumped again and caught it this time. 'Piece of cake!' he panted, his legs swinging. 'Now watch!' Hand over hand, Tarzan fashion, he began to swing backwards out towards the end of the branch. As he did so, the branch began to bend under his weight. Jolian turned to look at her cat, and understood at last. Perched on a smaller limb of Jem's branch, Yaffa was dipping down out of the sky as the boy's weight forced the bough down.

'Jem, you genius!' Beside her, Kyle caught at the twigs of Yaffa's branch and pulled it towards them. Standing on tiptoe, Jolian peeled a wild-eyed cat from her perch, brought her down at arm's length, dangling by the scruff of her neck, her paws swiping the air for a clawhold. 'You turkey!' She dropped her on the windowsill and Yaffa bounded into the room, tail stiff with outrage.

'Jem, you're brilliant!' Jolian told the boy as he flopped down on the roof just above her, his feet dangling. 'She'd have been up there till Christmas if you hadn't come along.'

Jem's offhand shrug utterly failed to hide his pleasure. If Fletch could just see him like this! Was this all he needed? 'All in a day's work,' he said modestly, his face glowing.

'Does McKay's Feline De-treeval Service take payment in brownies?' she enquired politely.

'You better believe it, lady!'

While Jolian set out the plates for the brownies, Jem kneeled by the table, one hand carefully extended towards Yaffa. Huddled under a chair, the Siamese crouched lower, her ears flattened. 'Hiya, gorgeous!' he crooned, making no move to touch her, his fingers steady. One of Yaffa's ears relaxed a trifle—swivelled towards him and then back again.

Jolian shot him a nervous glance, but said nothing. Jem was making the right approach, but Yaffa might be too riled to except it right now. Beside Jem, Kyle stood with his hands back in his pockets, staring down at the open cheque-book she'd been cursing when Yaffa first yowled for help. *Nosy kid!*

'You made a mistake here,' he said suddenly.

'I know, it won't balance. I——' Jolian looked up from cutting the brownies, her eyes widening. No pencil, no calculator—Kyle was doing that in his head? She walked over to stand beside him, frowning.

'Check number 302,' he mumbled, nodding down at the cheque-book. 'Your balance should be 987.69 there. You forgot to carry one.' His eyes flicked on down the column of figures. 'And there—you did it again in the cents column this time. That last figure is ten cents too high, but taking into account the first mistake, your final balance this page is . . . 681.14.'

Jolian picked up a pencil, scribbled the sum next to her own figure, then looked up again, her eyebrows lifting. 'You're sure?' He had to be pulling her leg.

His look of surprise answered her question. He was sure. Reddening under her gaze, Kyle nodded stiffly, turned and wandered aimlessly into the living room, his shoulders hunched.

Jem stood up from the floor, Yaffa cradled gingerly in his arms. 'If it's numbers, he's sure, Jolian,' he confirmed. He shot a mischievous, triangular smile at his friend and the next words were raised for his benefit. 'He can't spell his own name the same way twice, but he knows his numbers.'

'Lucky for you I can't,' Kyle growled, ducking his head. He wandered over to her workshop doorway and leaned there, studying the room intently.

And what do you make of this, my dear Watson? As she brought their plates into the living room and set them on the side table, Jolian could make nothing of it, nothing that made sense. She glanced at her watch. 'Oops! We've got to watch something.' She gestured at the small television set housed in the bookshelf across the room. 'See if you can find *My Brother's Keeper* for me, will you, Jem?' She started for the kitchen, wondering if boys drank skim milk. If she poured it out of their sight, they'd probably never notice the difference.

'You watch soap operas?' asked Jem, sounding vaguely disappointed.

'Not usually, no,' she called back, pouring the milk. 'But my business has a contract with this show. We supply all the jewellery the stars wear, and there's going to be a close-up of a necklace I designed, in a dance scene. I've been waiting for this for ages.' Her eyes lit on the cake pan and the rest of the brownies. That was silly, serving teenage boys one brownie apiece. If she brought them all out, they would eat them all. And Jem was looking a bit thinner, wasn't he? She ought to be giving him a tuna sandwich and a salad, not junk food. He probably hadn't looked a carrot in the eye since he ran away. Oh well. She picked up the knife.

When Jolian returned to the living room, Jem and Kyle were huddled in front of the set, their eyes riveted to the struggling figures there. That couldn't be *Keepers*, surely? The boys didn't look up as she came to stand behind them. On the screen, one man went down with a grunt and the other crouched above him, fists cocked. Jolian laughed softly. 'Jon Corey in *Blue Riders*. My God, I loved that man! I guess I cried for a month when he died—me and every other teenage girl in the country.'

The camera was moving in for a close-up of that fabulous face—heroically battered for this scene. A line of blood trickled down from the corner of his mouth, and his lips tilted up in that angular, heart-wrenching grin. He whipped the blond hair out of his eyes. 'Get up, Dawson, we're not done yet!' he rasped.

As Jem hit the knob, the picture contracted to a point of light and blinked out. His hand stayed on the knob, twiddling it slowly back and forth. The blond head below her was unnaturally still, fixed on that blank screen. 'Jem?' Jolian touched his shoulder.

'He drank himself to death,' he murmured, unmoving.

Kyle shot him a nervous look, then glanced up at Jolian and down again. He cleared his throat.

If she could just see Jem's face! 'I guess he did,' she agreed gently, utterly bewildered. 'He was one of those shooting star kind of people—four films on the way up, two on the way down, all gone in five short years.' She crouched down behind Jem, put a hand on his shoulder. 'What's the matter, Jem?'

He shook his head rapidly and Jolian gasped as she glimpsed the colour of his cheeks—greeny-white. 'Nothing!' he muttered.

'He doesn't like blood,' Kyle said clearly beside them. He blushed as Jolian turned to stare at him. 'He's a real chicken-heart when it comes to blood, right, Jem?'

'Right,' Jem murmured. 'That's it.' His grin was ghastly. *'Yuk!'*

Kyle glanced at his watch. 'You know, Jem, I've got a——'

'Right.' Jem cut that statement with some of his old

vitality. 'I know.' He smiled again for her, almost got it right this time. 'I'm feeling sort of sick,' he told her frankly. 'I think I better go too.'

And he was not to be dissuaded. It was all Jolian could do just to get them to take a package of brownies along. His colour returning, Jem promised to call her soon, and seemed to mean it. At the door, Jem stopped to give Yaffa's tail a gentle tug, and dodge her half-hearted swat. He grinned at Jolian, started to speak, then shrugged. ''Bye,' he said shyly, and followed Kyle's clumping footsteps down the stairs.

'And what do you make of *that*, Yaffa?' she murmured. Scurrying into her bedroom, she peeped out of the window at the street. She caught a glimpse of a shiny, ten-speed bike overloaded with two boys wobbling around the corner, Kyle's legs flapping and then folding as he pedalled, Jem hanging on behind, his mirror glasses gleaming, his baseball cap on crooked. 'What in heaven's name do you make of all *that*?'

Fletch, as you can see, I'm gone. Won't be back this weekend. I saw Jem this morning—Friday—and learned the following things:

1. He has a friend—Kyle Taylor. sixteen—seventeen; blond; *not* a street kid, whatever he is; *very* good at math.

2. I think Jem is staying within ten minutes' bike ride of this house.

Jolian tapped the pencil absently on the margin of the paper, doodled a quick star with a chequered comet tail. Even sticking to facts, it was amazing how much she had to tell Fletch. It would be so much easier in person . . . Easy? Ha! She squeezed her eyes shut, shook her head, and went back to the list.

14. Is Jem bothered by blood?

She glanced at her watch. Three-thirty. *Got* to get out of here. If Fletch followed his pattern so far, he could be flying into town any time today or tomorrow.

19. Please don't call me again. Please. If you have more questions, tell your detective to come see me. I'll talk to him.

Her pen hesitated, touched the paper, and lifted again, leaving a tentative mark where the complimentary close should be written. Four letters and a comma—'love',—so easy to feel and so useless to write. Fletch didn't want that from her, whatever he wanted. She transformed the mark into a quick sketch—a small bird winging away. She penned in a 'J.' below it, folded the message and dropped it in the envelope.

Cat feeder loaded with dry food? Check. Two bowls of water set out? Check. Toothbrush, clothes, sketch pads, one silver ring to finish for her father, a book, all the provisions for a weekend on the lam from Fletch? Check.

'Tell him "hi" for me if he knocks,' Jolian instructed the cat. She locked the door, then tacked the note to it, stood staring at it absently. Thank God Katy was going to Maine this weekend with her tofu man; the loan of her apartment near the hospitals was a life-saver. Fletch would never find her there. But what would she do next weekend—Al's couch? Don't think about it. Get through one day at a time. *You can't miss what*—Jolian squared her shoulders, picked up her night bag and trudged down the stairs. *You can't.*

On Monday morning there was an angry, neglected cat behind her door, and a new note tacked to its surface. He'd set it at his own eye level, jamming the tack in so hard that she broke a fingernail when she stood on tiptoe to pry it loose. Ignoring Yaffa's desolate cries, she leaned back against the door to read it.

That won't do, Jolian. I need your help—*need* it.
So answer your phone, damn it!

                                                    Fletch

Unlocking the door, she scooped up Yaffa and
wandered down the hallway to her bedroom, dumped
cat and overnight bag on the bed. 'Need'—had Fletch
used that word on purpose? His jewellery box gleamed
on her bureau; she opened it idly, her hands caressing
the different colours of wood as they unfolded. But
'need your *help*,' he had said, not 'need *you*' . . . She slid
open the secret drawer, stared down at the pearl, shut
the drawer again quickly. 'I pay my debts,' he'd also
said, and, 'I don't need anybody.' Sadly she closed the
box again and stood holding it, her hands cupping its
elegant curves, her eyes distant. No, he'd made it
perfectly clear from the start. What Fletch felt for her
was not love, and he had no intention of giving love a
chance to grow between them. In the few times they'd
met, he had been so careful to keep her at arm's length,
never asking about her past, never asking what she
hoped for the future. All he had wanted from her was
the present. Fletch didn't want, wouldn't let himself
need the rest of her.

'Well, I need you, Fletch,' she murmured, setting his
box down with gentle fingers, 'but I can't talk to you
. . . Not till it stops hurting.' Maybe in a week or two
. . . Or a month . . . A year, maybe?

That night she took her own overnight shift at the
Hotline; on Tuesday night she unplugged the phone.
Wednesday night she taught the jewellery class, slept
again with the phone disconnected, and on Thursday Al
had someone he wanted her to meet.

Jolian dressed for the evening with care. Ostensibly
this was a business dinner, but there had been a certain
note in Al's voice . . . She chose a grey wool dress, a
soft, zip-front knit which gently skimmed her curves,

neither denying nor flaunting them, black slender heels, dark hose, a black, white and grey plaid shawl to ward off the unseasonable cold. A pair of her own earrings— a simple, dangling leaf-like design which had always been one of their best sellers—completed the outfit. Studying herself in the mirror as she would have criticised one of her own designs, Jolian sighed slowly. She would do. She looked a bit hollow-cheeked and dark-eyed nowadays, but with her hair down and curling around her cheeks and shoulders, the underfed look was softened to fashionable thinness. All she needed was a smile. She tried one on and winced. Must be out of practice. She scowled—*that* was easy.

'Cheer up, Jolian,' she told her reflection. 'You've got no problems . . . You could always have one leg. Or two heads . . . Or four Siamese cats.' Or no son. Or no lover, *but you can't miss what you've never had, so stop feeling SORRY for yourself! Cheer up.*

The late afternoon sky had a lowering, thick look to it, a grey, woolly blanket snagged in the black fingertips of the trees along the river. There was snow in that sky . . . The joggers along the footpath bobbed like steam-powered toys today, white puffs trailing back from their wind-reddened cheeks.

Driving across the bridge, she divided her attention between the traffic and an eight-man racing shell. In the distance, it looked like a water-bug, some sort of sea-going centipede, the heads of its crew black vertebrae above the flashing dark legs of the oars. Between her and the shell, a small figure leaned over the bridge railing, Red Sox cap pulled low, red plaid pants bright in this blue-grey landscape. In the rear-view mirror she caught the glint of his glasses. Jem, and there was no way she could stop on the bridge. It was too late even to honk.

She found a place to park on Beacon Street. He would be gone, she told herself as she legged it back up the long curve of the bridge, ignoring the honks and leers from the passing cars. He would be gone; it was too cold. He would have moved on by now. Her eyes caught a patch of red in the distance.

Pushing off from the parapet, Jem turned away from her, trudging across the river in the direction of M.I.T. and Cambridge beyond. 'Jem!' she called, but there was no way he would hear her. Head down, hands in pockets, he wandered a few feet, then stopped to stare upriver across the slow-moving traffic. Following his gaze, Jolian saw another shell stroking towards the bridge. She shortened her long-legged, killing stride as Jem turned back to lean over the parapet, and came up on him slowly, fighting for breath. Nothing like the casual approach.

As she moved into hailing range, Jem turned. He was a long moment in recognising her, and then the bill of the baseball cap jerked up. His triangular, flashing grin answered her own laugh and then vanished. She saw his chin drop as he looked down at the book in his hands, then up to her again and, for a moment, she thought he might run. He flicked a glance over his shoulder towards the shore, but then, turning back to face her, he shrugged sheepishly.

Stopping, Jolian brushed the windblown hair back from her eyes and rearranged the shawl around her shoulders, giving him time.

Jem's rueful grin acknowledged her tact. Jamming—hiding—the spine of the hardcover book in his armpit, he came forward to meet her, his smile shyly apologetic now. 'Hi, Jolian.'

'Hi, stranger.' He needed a hug as much as Fletch did, probably more, but she didn't quite dare to give it. Reaching out, she gave the bill of his cap a gentle downward tug and he smiled again. 'You feeling better today?' But his cheeks looked too flushed, even given the river wind slicing across the bridge.

Jem nodded briskly. 'Yup, I'm fine.'

Taking hold of the sideframe of his fun-house glasses, Jolian raised her eyebrows, asking his permission. He shrugged and, lifting them gently off his face, she studied his eyes—a paler blue than her own, and much too bright. The backs of her fingers laid against his cheek told her nothing, his skin was too chilled. 'I think you've got a fever, friend,' she told him as he turned away from her, leaned against the railing to stare down at the river just below.

He shrugged and Fletch's hard smile crept into place. 'I'm okay,' he told the water huskily.

She came to lean beside him, shivered as her forearms touched the iron railing. And him with no jacket, just that stupid M.I.T. sweatshirt again. She returned the glasses; he gripped them blindly as they touched his hand. 'Jem, do me a favour,' she urged.

His eyes came back to her and he gave her his own smile this time. 'If I can.

'Show me how far you can throw those stupid glasses and then go home.'

'Home ...' Jem mused, as if the word were unfamiliar. He shook his head slowly, his eyes glittering.

With both hands Jolian captured the wisps of hair swirling around her cheeks, holding them back at the nape of her neck. 'Home to Ralph and a father who cares about you. Cares a lot more than he can say.'

Jem shook his head slowly again and turned back to the water. 'Can't ...' The wind caught the soft word and whirled it away. 'I can't.'

'Why not?' she demanded, fighting the urge to grab and shake him. 'I don't understand, Jem—why not?'

The boy shivered, hugging himself, and leaned further over the bridge railing. 'Because I went to New York.' He laughed bitterly, shaking his head. 'And I thought I had it bad before that ...' His lips were trembling now, and not with the cold. '*God*, I wish I'd never gone to New York!'

'But——'

Below them the empty air seemed to explode. Slashing out from under the bridge, the bow of the racing shell burst into view, revealing one straining face after another. Snarling grunts, steam hissing through white clenched teeth, eight big men leaned back against the oars as the shell shot forward and away—a fabulous, surging insect-machine, its voice the jubilant cries of the cox in the stern as he chanted the stroke in a rhythmic, pleading, brutal demand.

Mouths open, they watched it go, then turned to each other, laughing their delight.

'*Some day* . . .' Jem murmured. The words had the fierce dreaminess of a vow. He turned again to stare after the boat, his eyes fever-bright. 'Some day . . .'

It would be too brutal to remind him that rowing was a college sport, and that runaways seldom went to college. Perhaps the thought occurred to him as well; she watched the joy fade from his face.

'Jem——'

'Don't,' he said gruffly, turning back to face her. 'Please don't.' He smiled pleadingly. 'Let's talk about something else, like . . . like how great you look in a dress.' His flush deepened, climbed up to the ears.

Jolian laughed softly. 'Jem, any guy who can change the subject with such class will go far! And why is it men always prefer dresses?'

'Legs,' he twinkled, looking even younger than fourteen with that mischievous grin.

She shook her head mockingly. 'You're your father's son, Jeremy McKay.'

His smile vanished. He shivered again, hugging himself, got a better grip on the book he had been concealing all this time, his eyes studying her frankly. 'You like him, don't you, Jolian?'

It was her turn to hide. She turned back to the
railing. The two shells had found each other, were
working upstream again along the far bank, side by
side, distance turning the gut-wrenching duel to an
effortless ballet. 'Yes,' she managed finally. 'Yes, I do.'
She shrugged and turned back to him, met his troubled
gaze. 'But I guess most women do.'

'Yes,' he murmured, his eyes scanning her face as if he'd
never seen her before. 'I wish . . .' He sighed and shook his
head. 'Just don't let him . . . get to you . . . hurt you.'

A little late for that advice, friend. Her teasing smile
was probably not too convincing, but it would have to
do. 'Hey, I'm a big girl, Jem!' Her eyes flocked to a
burly figure loping up the sidewalk towards them and
back to Jem's frown.

'Yeah, but——'

'Shadow!' Jem reeled as the taller boy caught his arm
and spun him around. 'I've been hunting all over for
you, man! You've gotta help me!'

'Hey, Grover, gimme a break!' Jem shrugged his arm,
jerking backward, but failed to break that fervent grip.
'Can't you see I'm busy?' He jerked his chin her way,
scowling at the boy—young man, really—who topped
him by nearly a foot.

Grover's eyes shifted to her. Jolian watched them
blink, widen and swing slowly back to Jem. 'I've gotta
party tonight. You've gotta help me.' Grover's eyes
flicked back to her face, as if to confirm she was still
there. She was. Mystified, he turned back to Jem again.
'Is this for real?' he blurted, flipping a thumb in her
direction.

'Are *you* for real?' Jem bristled. This time he broke
the hold on his shoulder. 'Look, can we talk later?'

'But I've got a party tonight,' Grover moaned. His
eyes switched to Jolian and his face changed to an
ingratiating leer. 'Want to go to a party, by the way?'
He waggled his eyebrows suggestively.

Jolian laughed and shook her head. 'I have a date, thank you.'

His mournful nod said he'd only expected as much, and Grover turned back to Jem. 'Look, Shadow, you've gotta help me, I need three——'

'Wait a minute,' Jem cut in. An octave deeper and it would have been his father speaking. 'Jolian, will you excuse us, please?' He waited for her nod and then dragged his companion down the bridge out of earshot.

Fascinated, she watched the debate, Jem's gesture of outrage as Grover tried to give him a bill—she couldn't see what—the older boy's reluctant surrender of a second bill, and the final agreement. Drugs, it had to be drugs. Grover would be a freshman in college, possibly a sophomore. *Drugs and parties—Jem what have you got yourself into?* Fletch would throw a fit. She watched Jem force the book, whatever it was, on Grover, and send him on his way by sheer force of personality, a terrier routing a reluctant Great Dane.

As Jem returned to her, she could see the energy he had summoned to deal with Grover seeping out of him even as he walked. He was definitely coming down with something, ought to be out of this wind. She shivered and pulled the shawl closer around her. 'The shadow?' she asked as he stopped before her, 'as in *What evil lurks*——'

'*in the hearts of men?*' he nodded, grinning.

'*The Shadow Knows!*' They chanted it together, pulling off a sinister cackle at the end of it which would have done the real invisible hero proud.

'You've got a date?' asked Jem, his laughter fading. 'With my . . . my father?'

She shook her head, stifling the sudden pain that it was not so. 'With my business partner and a woman we're interviewing for a job as a sales representative.'

'I've made you late,' he observed with that consideration that was so rare in a fourteen-year-old.

He shivered again, bracing himself against it but unable to hide the spasm.

'Yes, and you're freezing to death. Jem, just tell me one thing?'

His eyes were uneasy and far too bright. 'Yes?'

'Things may be going okay for you now, but what will you do for Thanksgiving? For Christmas? What about poor Ralph stuck in a hotel? What about your father, running himself ragged between here and Chicago?'

Jem's head drooped slowly under the barrage, the bill of his cap shielding his face as he stared down at his toes. She could just see his lips trembling, searching for a smile, a word, some answer to her hammering. God, if she made him cry, would he ever forgive her? He shrugged weakly and did not look up. 'What——' He swallowed and tried again '*What* was the question?' He almost got a twinkle into it.

Jolian laughed and caught his shoulders, gave him an exasperated shake as he looked up at last, his eyes swimming even as he smiled. 'The question was, will you come to brunch tomorrow at my place, Jem? Please?' Tomorrow they were going to have a talk—a real talk.

'Brunch?'

'You know, the meal you eat after breakfast and before lunch?' she teased, releasing him gently.

'Yeah, I know, Dad used to take me out for one on Sundays. I'd always starve by eleven . . .'

'We'll make this an early brunch, then,' she said decisively. 'Nine-thirty all right? Now just say yes and get out of this wind!'

'Yes.' He shivered again.

'Promise?' She backed up a step. Lord, was she late!

'Promise,' he nodded.

'Okay, see you then, Jem.' She backed away a few more stops, reluctant to leave him like this. 'And, Jem?'

The bill of the baseball cap lifted in question.

'Take two aspirins as soon as you can, and two more at bedtime.' She waited for his smile, then turned and hurried back across the long, cold curve of the bridge.

'Jolian, thank you.' The girl reached across the table to give her a quick, firm handshake. 'It's been a pleasure.'

'It certainly has.' Jolian smiled up at her. Lord, she was tall! 'And we'll let you know as soon as we can.'

Karin nodded and turned to Al, her look of friendly poise softening ever so slightly. If Jolian had not been waiting for it, she would have missed it. 'Goodnight, Al.'

Al's red beard jerked slightly, as if he had been some place else, had just landed with a *bump* at this candlelit table in a tiny Italian restaurant. 'You're . . . you're sure you can't stay, Karin?'

She shook her head slowly, smiling. 'This party's been planned for weeks, Al. I've got to go—I'm late as it is.'

He watched her out of the door, his yellow eyes unblinking, and Jolian seized the moment to signal their waitress. 'Could we have one of these, please?' She tapped the wine list, but her discretion was wasted on Al. He was decidedly elsewhere.

His eyes blinked rapidly, registering the girl's departure at last, and he turned her way, starting as he met her affectionate grin. 'Well, what do you think?' he asked quickly, groping in the side pocket of his rumpled jacket.

'I think they'll call in the fire department if you smoke that thing here!'

'Oh . . .' He stuffed the pipe back in its home, nodding meekly. 'Well, what do you think?' he asked again.

'Well . . .' The impulse to tease was irresistible, 'she has lovely, lovely—' Jolian paused, watching him nod in agreement before he'd even heard the rest, '—hands,' she finished, laughing at his blink of surprise. 'And she uses them beautifully when she talks. I could just picture our rings and bracelets waving under the buyers' noses while she explains why they've got to carry the Quicksilver Collection.'

'She has pretty ears, too,' Al interposed.

Jolian threw back her head and laughed. 'And she even has a neck,' she agreed. 'She can wear it all, earrings, necklaces—the girl's versatile!'

'C'mon, Jolian, cut it out. What do you think?' Al hunched forward, his thick, clever fingers tapping the tablecloth between them.

The waitress arrived with the Asti Spumante at that moment. 'I'll open it,' Jolian told her, lifting the bottle from its bucket of ice. 'Well ...' she peeled back the golden foil, flicking a glance at his anxious face, 'I think ...' Her fingers curled round the cork, inching it slowly out of the bottle. It came all at once with a good, clear *Pop*! 'I think you're cured!' she laughed triumphantly.

The bottle was foaming over. She swung it towards him and he lifted his glass automatically. 'Congratulations, partner!' she told him, splashing his glass full. It had been a long two years since Nancy had left him. As she filled her own glass, she offered a short, fierce prayer that this one would be different. But Karin would be; she could tell already. Nancy had never looked at Al like this girl did. Nancy had never looked past the end of her own selfish, elegantly-bobbed little nose.

Al's mouth was still open. She clinked glasses with him, bringing his eyes back to the present. 'Drink, friend,' she reminded him gently. 'You've found your cure.'

His beard bristled as a wide, boyish grin spread slowly. 'Do you think so?' he wondered.

'I think so. Cheers.' Jolian touched glasses with him

again and then drank this time. The wine was so cold it
hurt. Tilting her head back, she shut her eyes and let the
bubbling pain spread out along her veins, wishing she
could smash the empty glass to the floor, stamp it to
splinters. That was what Asti tasted like tonight,
smashed, frozen glass—shards of crystal. God, she was
a jerk to be so envious of Al's luck! She looked down to
find his eyes on her, wide awake now under his bushy
eyebrows. She smiled and held her glass out for a refill.
'So let's get smashed!' she said gaily.

He tilted the bottle tantalisingly, just beyond her
reach. 'You'll leave your car in the parking garage, take
a cab home?'

'Oh, c'mon, Al!'

'I'm thinking of the party you left six years ago,
Jolian, swearing you were going to drive to the top of
Mount Washington.'

She winced. 'But I never——'

'Right, but Sandy and Rob and I did, hoping to save
your fool neck! You ended up out on the Cape
somewhere, watching the sun rise, as I recall.'

'I was nineteen then, for Pete's sake!'

'And you get just as reckless nowadays when you
drink too much.' Al waved the bottle sternly. 'Cab and
Asti or home to bed like a good girl?'

Jolian sighed and held out her glass again. 'Cab,
Grandfather.'

'Cheers, then.'

'Cheers.'

They sipped it this time, studying each other. Al's
eyebrows jumped—a bristly shrug. 'So we've settled
me. 'I'm going to live happily ever after, after all—as
easy as that.' He grinned wryly. 'Now what about you?'

She took another icy sip and licked her lips. 'What
about me?'

'C'mon, Jolian, I've been waiting for two weeks for
you to say something. You've just about doubled your

design output, you're laughing more than ever, but one note's gone flat somehow, and you look like you might break if you tripped and fell . . . Who's the rat?'

'He's not a rat!' She smacked her glass down so hard the wine sloshed over.

'Hush! Hey, cool it, Jolian!' Al glanced around sheepishly, smothered her drumming fingertips with a big hand. 'Cool it . . . Okay, he's not a rat, he just makes you feel awful. He's a swell guy.'

'Damn it, Al, he's just been hurt. He's had rotten luck—a lousy childhood and a lousier marriage, and he's just so determined not to let himself in for any more bad luck, he can't recognise good luck when it falls in his lap!'

Al sighed and shook his head slowly. 'The good luck being you?'

'The good luck being me,' she agreed defiantly. 'I could make him happy, I know I could.' She squeezed her eyes shut, a picture of Fletch laughing branded across her eyelids.

'Some people don't want to be happy,' Al warned her softly, pouring himself another glass full.

'You're really cheering me up, Al. You really are,' she said bitterly, holding her glass out for a refill.

'Sorry.' But he shook his head at her glass. 'You don't want to get drunk, Jolian. You want to go home, take a shower, go to bed, sleep late, and get up fresh tomorrow. Have a bike ride and then come see me for lunch and let's talk.' He poured the last of the wine into his glass, downed it with the casual disregard for alcohol of a very large man. 'Now that is Dr Frasier's tried and true prescription. I've been there.'

She sighed. Yes, he had been there. Would it take two years to get over Fletch? And this had started out as a celebration of Al's recovery, not her woes, hadn't it? *Cheer up, Jolian. You can't miss——* 'Okay, doctor, we'll do it your way.'

She let him order her a cab at the front desk. They were stepping out into the street when the waitress caught them. 'Miss, is this your hat?'

Jolian laughed and took it from her. 'No, but I know whose it is.' She twirled the sky blue beret under Al's nose. 'You're in luck tonight, friend!'

His big hand closed over the soft wool with a delicate, almost reluctant touch as he met her eyes.

'Where did Karin say that birthday party was?' she prompted him, smiling.

'Revere Street,' he answered. 'I know the guy that's giving it, but don't you think it would be barging in?'

'Absolutely not!' Jolian hooked her hand through his elbow and started marching him towards the corner. How could anyone this big be so shy? 'It's a cold night, the lady needs her hat, and ... why don't you tell her she's hired while you're at it?'

Al stopped short and turned to face her. 'You're sure?'

Smiling, Jolian glanced over her shoulder towards the restaurant. One car had pulled into the kerb just down the block, but it wasn't her cab. 'I'm sure she'll be an excellent sales rep. It's up to you, Al. Do you want to mix business and pleasure?'

He rubbed the beret slowly across his bearded cheek, inhaling the scent of it in a deep, slow breath, and nodded fiercely. 'Yes!' Grabbing her, he pulled her forward into a big exuberant bear-hug and nodded against her hair again. 'Yes, I do!'

'So go tell her she's hired,' she laughed up at him, patting his shoulders encouragingly.

'All right.' Al sucked in his breath, gathering his courage. 'All *right*.' He kissed the tip of her nose. 'And you tell your rat, next time you see him, that he's a fool!' Spinning away, he started down the street with big, determined strides. By the time he reached the next corner, he was running.

Jolian laughed softly, shaking her head. It was better than crying. As a snowflake touched her cheek, she lifted her face to the night sky, waiting for the next kiss of winter.

'Congratulations,' a whisky-smooth voice drawled behind her, 'on your speedy recovery!'

CHAPTER EIGHT

'*Fletch!*' Spinning towards the source of that voice, Jolian caught her heel and nearly went down. Hands clamped around her upper arms. Bruising as they took her weight, they yanked her up against his solid, unmoving warmth. Fingers outspread across his chest, she leaned against him, staring up into that dark, unsmiling mask. He was real. This was not just one more dream: he was real. She pulled a deep, shaking breath and flexed her hands, drawing her fingertips across the roughness of his dark coat, his heart going like a jackhammer beneath it—angry as hell, but real, under her hands. What else really mattered tonight? Her soft, jubilant laughter stopped as he shook her savagely, his breath hissing.

Even angrier than she'd thought . . . and the shaking had made her dizzy. *Talk, Jolian. Break this deadly silence.* She shook her head to shake the curls off her cheeks and then wished she hadn't. 'Fletch, what are you doing he——'

'God damn you!' His mouth came down hard against her lips and then froze even as she responded. He thrust her away again and held her off from his warmth a few inches, his eyes glittering. 'Your hair smells like your friend's pipe, and you've been drinking.' One corner of his mouth curled in disgust.

She didn't need this. Didn't need it at all. Bad enough that he was stomping back into her life, he didn't have to kick in the door with his stormtrooper boots as well! 'You . . . are . . . *hurting* . . . me, Fletch.' She ground out the words carefully as she shook her hair back again, her eyes widening with her growing anger. She didn't

164

need this. *She* was the one with a right to be angry, not Fletch!

'So join the club,' he breathed, but the brutal grip eased and her heels could touch the pavement at last. His eyes moved over her, missing nothing from her toes to her throat in a slow survey that warmed her body from the inside out. She was suddenly aware of chilled skin stretching tight over a core of fire, fire that was not all anger, her breasts swelling against the thin wool of her dress. And those green-gold eyes missed nothing. His mouth lifted in a bitter half-smile as his fingers stirred on her arms. 'Join the club, silky cat.'

That he could light her with just one look—damn his eyes, and damn her body for responding like this! But what had he said, join the club? 'How—I don't understand—how have I hurt *you*, Fletch?'

'With a good sharp kick in the pride.' His mouth twisted in savage self-mockery. 'The tenderest part of the male anatomy.' His hands tightened again, swaying her forward to brush against the hard length of him, a body to body caress. 'Two weeks ago you loved *me*—so you said. And now I suppose you love *him*.' His chin jerked in the direction that Al had taken. 'I suppose that's where you were last weekend—in his bed? And those nights when I tried to phone you and no one was home—in his bed, silky cat?' His lips touched the point of her upturned chin, moved slow, warm and hard along her jaw till he breathed in her ear. 'And those nights when the phone was disconnected—did you take him into *your* bed, silky? All for that magic word I wouldn't give you? All for love?' Fletch's hands slid slowly around her shoulders and his arms tightened, surrounding her, locking her into this trap of muscle and bone and rushing blood. His lips moved to brush her mouth and then withdrew an inch, hovered just above her as brutal as any threat. 'So do you love *him* this week?' he jeered.

Dizzy. Her heart trapped by the rhythm of his now, beating too fast, hurting her breast. Damn him. 'What if I do?' she whispered against his lips. 'What's it to you?'

He brushed her mouth again, a touch like that tender, measuring stroke of the cat-o'-nine-tails before the first real blow. 'Call it morbid curiosity, my little alleycat!'

Alley——! She'd show him some claws if she could just free her hands! His bitter smile widened as he read her struggles correctly and his hold tightened, pinning her forearms against his chest, crushing the last of the air from her lungs. 'You're ...' She stopped, gasping for breath, '*you're* a fine one to talk ... you, with ... all your women!'

'All my——' Fletch laughed incredulously, and his brows slanted up in a derisive shrug. 'Well, there's a difference there, silky.' His grip eased again as she stopped fighting him. 'I call *that* what it is—fun and games. No more, no less. You won't find *me* tossing around fine words like love. *I* don't take that word in vain.'

Lips parted in astonishment, she stared up at him. What did he want? Did he want her to plead her love one more time, insist it was real so he could reject it again? But his mouth came down at last, sweeping speculation before it, bruising her lips, forcing her head back, turning the world into a dizzy, spinning airless sensation of heat and darkness. Nothing was real but the strength of his arms, the pressure of his lips, his breath warming her cheek and rising in white steam around them. The world contracted to this moment and these lips, nothing more. Her fingers curled into his jacket as she held on for dear life.

And then she could breathe again. Her mouth was her own. Shuddering, she ducked under his chin, leaned her forehead against the pulse in his throat, hiding from those punishing lips and inhaling the warm, clean smell of his skin.

But above her, Fletch still had words with which to wound. '—at least show some taste in your lovers, can't you?' he snarled against her hair. 'Choose one who'll see you home, not some clod who leaves you on the corner ... I could have been a mugger, coming up behind you like that!'

Too *much*! From somewhere she found breath to laugh, laughed in his face as he pulled her out from his neck to glare down at her.

'Thanks, but I'll take the mugging next time ... if it's all the same to you!' All muggers took was your money. They didn't stamp your heart on the sidewalk. Her laughter was suddenly too close to tears.

'Damn it, Jolian!' Fletch stared down at her, his lips curling despite the anger in his eyes. He shook her gently. 'Don't you dare have hysterics on me!'

'Wi-will if I want!' she gasped, squeezing her eyes shut against the tears.

'So you'll have them in my car, then. Let's go.' One arm curled around her waist and he turned towards the car at the kerb.

'No!' What was she doing, letting him back into her life, into her heart like this without a thought? Nothing had changed. She'd only have to live the pain all over again. 'No, I'm not going anywhere with you, Fletch!'

His arm tightened, holding her up as she stumbled, sweeping her along beside him. 'Grow a foot and I might bother to debate that with you.' They reached the car and he swung the door open, his smile mocking her helplessness. 'Otherwise, get in.'

Letting him back into her life—ha! She flashed him a bitter look as she sat and swung her legs into the car. But Fletch's eyes were on her bared knees, not her face. His breath hissed and he reached down, caught her thigh just above the knee, his fingers caressing the slippery smoothness of the dark nylon. Clenching her teeth over a wordless gasp, Jolian glared up at him, but her body arched with its own response as his fingers tightened.

'Silky . . .' he taunted softly, his smile a reckless promise as he met her outraged eyes. Fletch shut the door and strode around the front of the car with long, unhurried steps.

She should run for it—run for dear life. But her knees might not hold her, and Fletch was in the car already, the slant of his eyebrows warning her not to try it. She curled away from him into the corner next to the door, her arms folded, her eyes wide and defiant as the car swung into the traffic. A cab pulled into the kerb to take their place. And now what? What now, and what next? Taking a deep, shaking breath, she turned to watch him.

A pirate, that was what she'd thought the first time she met him, and Fletch looked the part again tonight with the street lights flashing and then fading across that hard half-smile. A smile that did nothing to hide the anger still blazing just beneath it. 'Where are you taking me?' she asked at last, keeping her voice soft. Music to soothe the savage breast.

'Home.' His eyes stayed on the street ahead. She watched his long fingers clench on the steering wheel, then slowly relax again.

So home, and then what, with him in this mood? And what did *she* want? It would help if she knew that. She wanted no more pain, but which was the worse pain? Losing him once again or having him here in this savage mood? She studied the hard, clean lines of his profile with hungry eyes. 'How did you find me?'

They turned on to the bridge before he answered. They would be home soon—too soon. 'By luck,' he growled at last. 'Which kind, I wouldn't know.'

Above them the clouds had cracked open, heaven's gates swinging wide to show the full moon, a silver magician ruling a curve of midnight blue. Fletch's eyes swept through her and past to stare out at the dark river, the moonshine and the lights of the town glittering on it like the scales on some magical snake.

'I'm staying at the Ritz Carlton, around the corner from where we met. I'd given up on finding you at home tonight, was coming back for something to eat when I saw you and your——' The car stopped for the light at the end of the bridge and Fletch swung around to face her, caught her chin in a bruising grip, his eyes raking her face.

'That hurts,' she said evenly, her eyes steady.

'Good.' But the grip eased. One of his brows lifted and he shook his head slightly, his eyes questioning.

'What?' she asked softly, dipping her chin so that her bottom lip brushed his knuckle.

She might have burned him. Fletch's fingers whipped away and he turned back to the wheel, cursing suddenly as a car honked behind them. They swung on to the parkway. Not far now. Too close, too soon, and what then? 'What?' she asked again.

Fletch shrugged tightly, his lips curling in an ironic smile. 'I'm just trying to figure out who and what you are, Jolian. I can't correlate the girl I left two weeks ago, crying on a couch, with the one who kisses dancing bears on street corners.' He shot her a rueful, savage look. 'I told you you'd live, not to live it *up*, dammit!'

It should have been funny, but it wasn't. Fletch didn't want her love, and he didn't want her to give it elsewhere, either. That made lots of sense, didn't it? She bit back an angry, bewildered laugh. And he thought she'd been living it up these last two weeks? It had barely been living! No, living it up was *his* style—Mr Fun and Games. No doubt Fletch had consoled himself with all kinds of games and fun!

'There's just one thing I have to know,' Fletch growled, turning into her street. The car glided into the kerb and he cut the engine off, turned to face her in the sudden quiet. 'Are you doing this to prove something to me—to make me sorry—or is this just your usual pace, a new lover every three weeks?'

'You—were—never—my—lover!' She ground the words out, her eyes flashing.

'So, that can be corrected, silky cat!' His face was murderous as he yanked her forward.

For a minute there, it was closer to war than love as they struggled against each other, their breath hissing. A war Jolian was losing as Fletch pressed her back over his encircling arm and his kiss pinned her there. Bruising and caressing her lips, he forced them apart for his pleasure, laughing his soft, wordless triumph into her mouth.

She was losing, but what a loss with his heart slamming against her breasts. As her eyes closed, strange patterns of light starred across the inside of her lids, red flares exploding above their battlefield. What a loss! Smiling into his kiss, Jolian suddenly relaxed. She had only been dreaming of these lips, these arms, this dark, angry face for two weeks—for all her life—so why fight them? As his face lifted above her at last, her fingers curled into the thick, wiry hair at the back of his neck and she pulled him down again.

'Damn you!' Fletch whispered, but this kiss was gentler.

Headlights swept across the car's interior as another car turned into the block. 'Damn.' Fletch lifted his head slowly, sighing against her cheek. His fingers ruffling slowly through her hair, he watched the car park, then turned back to her, his eyes black in the dim light. His other hand found her face, explored the hollow below her cheekbone down to her lips with one not quite steady fingertip, traced her shaky attempt at a smile. 'Let's go up,' he whispered.

Jolian forgot to turn on the light at the foot of the stairs. They went up through the dreamy, jagged darkness, the moonlight through the landing windows beckoning them higher. *And what do you want?* she asked herself as they climbed. *What?* But how could she think with Fletch one step behind her, his big, restless hand on her waist? How could she think with that hand stroking down the curve of her hip, sliding warmly, slowly down the back of her thigh as she moved? Hard enough to breathe in this dark, rhythmic ascent, much less think. The darkness was making her dizzy, but if she fell, Fletch would catch her . . . had caught her already.

At the door, her fingers were shaking too much to fit the key in the lock. Fletch didn't help. He came to stand just behind her, his fingertips exploring the curves of her breasts, her ribs, gliding slowly down across her stomach, pulling her back against the hard, urgent length of him. His touch was fever-hot and harder now as his hands curved round the front of her thighs. 'You *silky*!' he exulted in her ear as she leaned back against him. She could feel his heart pounding against her shoulderblade. As his lips burned the nape of her neck, sent slow, liquid fire spiralling down her backbone, she shuddered and threw a hand up, burying her fingers in his thick hair.

Somehow the key in her other hand found the lock and slid home with a soft *click*. But she couldn't turn it—shouldn't. Fletch reached past her and turned it for her.

This was crazy, begging for heartache, running to meet it with each of them wanting something so different. She turned in the tight circle of his arms, her lips parting, and his fingers found the slide of the zipper between her breasts.

She should say something. The moonlight lit his eyes as he looked down at her, waiting for her to speak, daring her to deny him, his eyebrow slanting up with the question.

And what did *she* want?

She wanted that zipper opened. Her breasts rose with a deep, sobbing breath, pressing up against the weight of his hand. And his answering smile was slow, slow as the deliberate, rippling *tick* of the zipper as he pulled the slide down.

Cold air on her skin and then hot hands . . . fever-hot hands sliding around her waist. Goosebumps rising everywhere and her nipples aching for his touch. She leaned against the wall, shuddering as his lips found her throat, burned their slow, melting way down her body to her wisp of a brassiere. Teeth bit her gently through the lace and her gasp echoed in the hallway. Her hands closed around the back of his head, pulling him closer.

Dizzy, dizzier and floating now as he lifted her, spinning as he turned to the door. His heart beating against her side as he held her, her whole body throbbing to its rhythm. Door opening then shutting behind them, Yaffa's half-purring complaint at Fletch's feet. Floating, so safe, so warm, as he moved across the room, her soft cry was a protest as Fletch set her on her feet by the couch. His hands closed on her shoulders, holding her away from his warmth.

Shadows of the branches outside the window zig-zagged across their bodies, breaking them into pieces of black and silver, all bits of the same shattered mirror in the moonshine. 'Silky cat!' Fletch whispered. His outspread fingers slid slowly up her throat, raked into her hair and combed it out to fall in a tousled, moonlit mane around her shoulders. 'Puritan!' he taunted as his hands came back to her dress, lifted it off her shoulders and dropped it. It slipped slowly down to her hips, clung to her hose for an instant and then slithered down her legs with a soft, electric crackle. 'Beautiful, crazy, faithless little alley cat!' His hands slid slowly round her hips, cupping them, pulling her up on her toes against him, his lips and then his teeth closing on the top of her shoulder.

Faithless! She shuddered and arched convulsively, pressing herself against him, frowning into his neck as his arms tightened around her. *Alleycat!* Yes, he wanted to think that—*had* to think it, didn't he? Her fingers found his back and she gave him just a taste of her claws, dragging them lightly down across the hard muscles to his waist. She smiled at his groan of pleasure.

'God, who *are* you, lady?' His lips teased her mouth, lifted away again. 'I don't even know you, tonight.'

I'm the one who loves you! She could say it, but he might just have the strength to walk out of that door again. Her fingers found the top button of his shirt. She leaned backwards, trusting herself to the hard arm around her waist as she fumbled with it. 'But you will,' she promised, her lips curving in a catlike, laughing smile with her secret. 'You will.'

After love's fever come dreams—sweet, tender dreams with Fletch's lips moving sleepily across her eyebrows and cheeks. She remembered his hands framing her face, their foreheads touching, and the question in his shadowy eyes. She smiled lazily, stretched purring beneath him, they fell asleep before she could answer it.

Through her lashes, the room was a patchwork of velvet greys when Fletch stirred at last and propped himself on his elbows. 'Where are you going?' she murmured, catching at his shoulders.

He stroked a curl off her forehead, ruffling her hair gently. 'I'm cold, kitten. Aren't you?'

Her smile was a drowsy, teasing yawn. 'No.'

She felt his soft laughter, rather than heard it. 'No reason you should be, I guess, with me for a blanket!'

'A comforter,' she corrected dreamily.

Laughing, Fletch rolled over and sat up. 'So come to bed,' he told her, his arms sliding beneath her. 'I want to comfort you again.'

This time it was like making love under water. Through her bedroom curtains, the first light of dawn washed their bodies with the luminous aquamarines of the seas off the Cape. Each motion, each caress in this thick, clear light was slowed to a dreamy, deliberate half-speed . . . a slow-motion ceremony of unspeakable, floating sweetness. A sweetness that brought the tears to her eyes. The soft ritual complete, she sank down beside him, hiding her face in the salty warmth of his shoulder, her body still rocking gently to the echoes of their waves.

She felt Fletch's deep, slow sigh as his fingers traced up her damp spine from hip to shoulder, twined slowly into the ripples of her outflung hair. 'Mmm.' She snuggled closer.

His fingers stopped their slow caress. 'Silky . . .'

'Mmm?'

'Who was that guy?'

She smiled against his skin. 'Al.'

His fingers tightened, pulling a little, and she squirmed restlessly. 'Are you lovers?'

Still hiding her face, Jolian shook her head against him. 'No . . . nor ever have been. We're friends . . .' She brought her hand slowly up from his waist, memorising the firmness of ribs and muscle, the tickling crispness of the hair across his chest.

Fletch rolled on to his side to face her suddenly, his fingers still buried in her hair. 'And why should I believe that?'

'Because . . .' She touched his cheek, almost smiling at its early morning roughness. 'Because I say it.'

His smile flickered for an instant, then it vanished into a wary blankness, but her hand on his face seemed to keep the worst of the hardness at bay. 'I lived with a woman—a wife—for seven years,' Fletch said carefully, 'who claimed she loved me . . . and all the while she was sleeping with anyone who asked.' His head twisted away from her fingers. 'So why the hell should I believe *you*?'

'Because I'm me,' she whispered, her fingers curling around the back of his neck. His muscles hardened, refusing to bend to her, so she stretched up to brush his tense mouth and then his jaw with her lips. 'And I *do* love you.'

Fletch's neck muscles jerked and went rigid beneath her hand. He tried to meet her reckless, tender smile with his own hard mask, couldn't manage it, and shook his head in sudden frustration. 'God, Jolian, don't do this to me!' Rolling away from her, he glared at the ceiling. 'I hurt just looking at you,' he growled, jaws clenching.

'Good,' she murmured. She wanted to hurt him. Hurt him all the way through. Any way to reach him was better than no way at all. She snuggled back against his shoulder, wondering if ice hurt when it melted. 'Good,' she whispered, and slept.

The gold-red of sunlight on her eyelids woke her, and her smile spread slowly as she remembered. Her hand crept across the rumpled sheets, seeking him . . . Not finding him. Something moved between her and the sunshine and she opened her eyes.

It was Fletch, staring out of the window, tension defining each muscle in his shoulders and hips with sculptural precision. And in that rigid, beautiful back Jolian could read the answer to all her hopes. She had fooled only herself last night.

His head swung towards her bureau suddenly, and then he followed his gaze, padding across the floor in long, silent strides. His box, that was what he had seen. Through gathering tears Jolian watched him unfold it, search it slowly, intently, as if the answer were hidden there somewhere.

He did not find it. She heard the slow hiss of his

breath as he shut the box at last, stood staring down at it.

His head turned. Green-gold eyes pinned her to the pillow, seemed to grow larger and more luminous as he approached the bed, unsmiling. And those eyes missed nothing. He caught a tear on his fingertip.

'I'd never hurt you, Fletch.' It was as close to begging as she could come. Too close. Her fingers slowly clenched on the sheet beneath her.

'I know,' he soothed. Warm and gentle, his hand covered her bare stomach, tensed slightly unconsciously cupping her flesh. 'Not on purpose. I know that now.'

'Not at all!' she flared, watching the muscles in his face slowly harden.

'Liz hurt my pride, silky cat—stamped it into the mud.' His hand glided slowly up her body, paused to fingertip her breast, and his eyes seemed to darken as her breathing changed. 'If *you* hurt me, it would cut deeper than that. You scare the hell out of me . . .'

'Fletch, I wouldn't——'

He shook his head quickly. 'Kitten, you're twenty-five. I'm thirty-seven—almost old enough to be your father.' He almost smiled as he used her words against her, put a quick hand across her parting lips. 'I'd wake up some morning to find you'd fallen for someone your own age.'

'You're crazy!' she cried against his fingers.

He shrugged tightly. 'Or you'd go dancing across the street in your lighthearted way one day and be run down by a truck.' Fletch shook his head ruefully. 'I don't want to risk it, Jolian. I have to travel light—no strings, no baggage, no looking back . . . no regrets.' He kissed her cheek and stood up. 'You knew that.'

Shutting her eyes, she nodded wearily. Yes, she'd known that all along. The only lies told had been the ones she had told herself.

His fingers touched her lips, seeking her smile. She

frowned. One fingertip pressed her bottom lip, rolling it out gently to steal a kiss. 'Go to hell!' she whispered against his touch.

Fletch laughed softly. 'I'll try the shower first.'

The only lies had been her own. Jolian repeated it savagely again and again as she brushed out her hair. It didn't help.

In the mirror, the shadows under her eyes looked like bruises. Her body felt bruised. It would remember Fletch's weight and exultant strength for days after he had gone. After he had gone ... She slithered into the blue silk caftan and padded to the kitchen. Give him coffee and get him out of here before she broke down. God, what a fool she had been!

She flashed a stormy glance over her shoulder as Fletch stepped from the bathroom. He was wearing his pants now, the dark hair curling damply across his bare chest. She turned back to the coffee cups.

Damp, muscular arms closed around her, wrapping her in his soapy, warm smell. 'God, what is it about you?' he growled, nuzzling the nape of her neck, his hands closing around her breasts.

Oh, no. No way. Never, ever, *never* again. She shuddered angrily and caught his left wrist, held it out for brisk inspection. 'Let's see, it's nine-thir——' she gasped. *Jem!* Oh, *God. Jem!*

And Fletch had felt her start. 'What's——'

Both their heads turned at the light *tap-tap* sounding on her door.

Oh, God—he would think she'd planned this. Think she'd betrayed him. Paralysed, Jolian stared at the door. The knock came again.

Fletch caught her shoulders and swung her around. One eyebrow rose dangerously as he saw her face. 'Who is it, kitten?'

She shook her head helplessly, her eyes enormous.

That old, hard smile was creeping back into place as

Fletch stared down at her. 'You're just full of surprises, aren't you, little cat?' he drawled finally. 'Is it Al? Or another one? How many of us are there, really, I wonder?' He let her go and turned towards the door.

'Don't, Fletch! Don't answer it! Please!'

'Just because you say so?' His whisper taunted them both. Shrugging her hands away, Fletch walked to the door, opened it casually, his face a smiling, ironic mask.

From the kitchen she saw the mask stripped away, baring first shock as his eyes widened. 'Jem,' he marvelled softly—and then a fierce, growing gladness. *'Jem!'*

So there was one person he did love.

'Son, wait!' Fletch slammed the door wide and dived into the hallway.

Numbly, Jolian came to the door. The boy looked shockingly frail leaning back against Fletch's big hands. Frail and sick—his face was green-white beneath the fever flush, his eyes blazing as he stared up at his father. His Red Sox cap lay crumpled beneath their feet. Jem swallowed, tried to speak, and then those shining eyes swept past Fletch to find her face. 'You tricked me,' he muttered hoarsely, his head beginning to shake in slow wonder. 'It was a trap. Come to goddamn *brunch.* You——'

'Jem! It wasn't like that!' Shaking her head desperately, Jolian took a step towards him and stopped. It was too late. 'I . . . time just got away from me,' she murmured helplessly . . . Too late.

Those glittering, pale blue eyes moved across her, missing nothing from her tousled hair to her bare feet beneath the silk robe. That feverish gaze lifted to his father, who had also turned to look at her, and then came back to her face. With a sick fascination she watched the comprehension dawning slowly in those wide eyes. 'I just bet it did,' he murmured absently. Contempt, and a kind of shame, were crowding close on its heels now. 'I just *bet* it did! So he got to you.

Even to you . . .' His teeth were chattering suddenly. 'Oh, hell. Oh, *hell*!' He twisted out of his father's hold and grabbed for his hat, stumbled and would have fallen but for Fletch's quickness.

Fletch caught his arm, gave him a gentle shake even as he steadied the boy. 'Watch your mouth, Jem. There's a lady——'

'*You*—you go to hell, too!' The hoarseness added years to Jem's voice, reminding her of someone . . . 'You can't tell me what to do!' he rasped, his fists clenching over his cap.

His brows a thunderous line, Fletch wrapped an arm around Jem's shoulders, started him towards the door and Jolian. 'Jem, I'm your father, I damn sure *will* tell you what to do, and you can start by apol——'

'You're not my father.' The strained words were deadly quiet.

'I——' Fletch stopped. Slowly he looked down at the boy. 'Liz told you that?' he asked ominously.

Jem twisted out of his hold, the tears starting at last. 'My father's a dead drunk named Jon Corey. You're . . . not . . . even . . . my——'

'*Jem* . . .' Fletch touched his shoulder, a suddenly tentative gesture. 'Jem, son . . .'

'I'm *not*!' Blinded with tears, Jem slammed his cap at their feet.

'The hell you're not!' Fletch caught his shoulders and spun him around to face him, bent down to his level, his eyes wide and determined. 'You *are* my son.'

'You're not even *listening* to me!' Jem's voice squeaked with frustration. 'My father was a drunk actor named——'

'I know that!' Fletch shook him urgently. 'So what, Jem? So *what*? You're my son in every way that matters!'

'You . . .' The boy stared at him, his teeth chattering a tiny, staccato rhythm in the silence. 'You . . . *know* that?' he whispered at last.

Fletch nodded earnestly, his eyes holding the boy's. 'She told me the day we got the divorce, Jem. So what? I'd raised you and loved you for six years. What was I supposed to do, turn it off that day? I needed a son as much as you needed a father.' Fletch's eyes flicked up to her face for a split second and then came back to the boy's.

'You *needed* me?' Jem murmured. 'But you never——'

Fletch gave him a gentle, rocking shake. 'Who the hell do you think I've been working so hard for all these years, pal?'

Jem was shaking his head again, the tears returning in a choking floodtide. 'But I didn't *care* about that, I just wanted . . . I just . . . wanted——'

Fletch straightened and pulled the unresisting boy against his chest. The dark head bent above the light, soothing the soft, pale hair with an unshaven cheek, his eyes glittering as bright as the boy's now. 'Jem, Jem, I know that now. I've been a fool . . . I said I was your father, I didn't say I was smart . . .'

They needed no audience. Jolian stepped slowly back from the doorway, but no one noticed her going. Yaffa crouched under the table, her tail and eyes enormous as Jolian collected her. 'And *we'll* cry in the bedroom,' she whispered into the soft fur.

She might even have slept. It seemed like hours before the door opened and shut, and the bed sagged under Fletch's weight. Yaffa shot off the pillow with a soft hiss as he pulled Jolian into his arms and hugged her. 'Thank you, kitten,' he murmured against her throat.

'Fletch, I didn't do that on purpose! He's got to understand that!'

He squeezed her soothingly, nodding against her skin. 'I think he does, Jolian. He's still upset right now, feels hurt and a little shy, but he does. I'll talk to him about it more when he calms down.'

'And he really is Corey's son?'

Fletch nodded ruefully. 'Can't you see it? It's getting stronger every day.' He rolled over on to his back and pulled her with him. 'That roadshow that came to Chicago was Corey's last play before Hollywood found him—and apparently he made the most of it. I think he laid every woman in the cast, from the ticket taker to the dowager; Liz was just the moron who got caught. She was one month pregnant when we married.' He shook his head restlessly, his beard prickling her skin.

'Did she know it then?' Jolian asked, her fingers sliding up to stroke the back of his head.

Fletch shrugged and burrowed closer into her shoulder. 'Don't know ... and don't even care any more, silky cat.' He sighed slowly, inhaling the scent of her skin. 'I've got to go. Can't keep him waiting, Jolian. I've done that too often ... We have to go get his gear, and I have to meet Kyle. Then it's back to Chicago and a doctor—fast.'

'The same Kyle I wrote you the note about?'

'Mm-hmm.' Fletch laughed softly into her hair. 'Kyle Taylor, early admissions student at M.I.T., mathematical genius and one-time junior counsellor at Jem's camp this summer. Jem's been sleeping on his floor and writing his English papers for him. And selling his literary services to half the freshmen in the dorm as well! My son, the entrepreneur!'

Fletch sat up suddenly and she watched his smile slowly fade as he met her eyes. He looked away, his green-gold gaze sweeping over the blue, clinging silk of her robe. He stroked her delicately with one fingertip, and his smile was almost sad as the fabric rustled.

'Silky cat,' he murmured. 'I don't know what to say ... I can't think straight around you—I——'

'Don't say anything,' she whispered, closing her eyes. 'Just *go* ...'

She heard his breath hiss and had to bite her lip to stop a sob. Warm and tickling, his lips brushed her eyelids. 'Goodbye, my silky. Thank you.' His hand curved round her breast, a feather light, heartbreaking touch, and then he was gone.

CHAPTER NINE

You can't miss what you've never had ... but when you've had it? What then? There was no forgetting him. Fletch had branded himself upon her, mind and body. Long after his scent was gone she would wake from dreams of his big, solid warmth to lie in the dark, the salt taste of his skin on her lips, her body echoing with the memories of his touch. The rustle of the sheets in her sleepless turnings brought back his laughing whispers, all the loving and hating names he had called her. She hung the blue silk robe in the back of the closet, hid his box away as well. Some day she would look at them again. Some day ...

The cold bronze of October faded to the colder steel of November—grey skies above slate roofs, the stark blacks of rain-drenched tree trunks. Winter was coming early this year. The morning frost on the leaves underfoot matched the ice in her heart. The only thing to do was to stay busy—work and wait for the springtime.

She brought designs to Al until he begged for mercy. She might have hung around the studio and helped with their production, but Al was too happy nowadays to be bearable. His assurances that this heartache would pass, that she would find a better love, were no comfort at all. She wanted Fletch, no other comforter.

She took on more commissions from the costume jewellery houses in Providence, drove her night class unmercifully. At home she rearranged the living room, washed the windows, cleaned the oven twice-weekly and even gave an outraged Yaffa the first bath of her life. Anything to kill the days.

The nights were unkillable . . .

The Hotline office became a second home. She must have talked to every last runaway in the country and she was no help to any of them. She was lost herself.

It was past midnight when Jolian parked the car outside her house, and stopped to stare up at the sky. She had taken the eight-to-twelve shift at the Hotline— should have stayed on for the overnight shift as well, let her replacement stay home in a warm bed. She would have got more use from hers than Jolian would tonight from *her* bed. *Stop feeling sorry for yourself*, she chanted automatically. It was a phrase worn smooth with use by now. *Cheer up, Jolian. Just look at that moon!*

A disc of hammered silver, the moon rode the skies like a pale ship as wave after wave of silver-grey cloud swept past it. The whole sky was on the move tonight, a moontide streaming from the south-east and the ocean to storm the land. She could almost imagine the cloud-waves thundering against the White Mountains to the north, cloud-spray shooting diamond-bright towards the stars.

The wind rattled the black branches above her and she shivered. It was a restless, wanting night. A night to just tear away and blow with the wind . . . A gust lifted the hair from her shoulders, tugged at her heart. There had been a full moon last month on that night. *Don't think about it! Don't you dare!* She shivered and went inside.

The moonlight came in at the window on the second floor landing. Fletch had met her here that day with the groceries. She could never sneak past this spot without remembering. Perhaps it was time to find a new apartment.

The stairs to the third floor were dark. She kept her eyes on the window above, a silver beacon at the end of her tunnel.

As she stepped on to the landing, the light went out—cloud-waves drowning the moon outside. She turned to the door and saw him, a black shadow seated on the dark floor, arms folded across up-bent knees, head tilted back against the wall.

There was only one man that it could be. Only one man in the whole world, as far as she knew. And this dizziness wasn't shock, whatever it was, Jolian thought as she sagged back against the banister, squeezing it till her hands hurt. It wasn't shocking to find Fletch here when he had been everywhere night and day for a month. It was just that, this time, he looked so real.

The moonlight returned, a silver line expanding slowly across the floor. It crept up those long legs, turned the tendons of those hands clenched round the elbows to slashes of black and silver. The moonlight climbed higher, lighting those wide shoulders, that strong neck and stubborn jaw, shining at last on that mouth she had once thought so beautiful, a mouth resting now in a grave, straight line. As the moon touched his eyes, she gasped—a tiny, echoing sound in this silence. They were open! He'd been so still, she'd thought——

Heart drumming in her ears, Jolian slid a hand backwards along the railing, found the cornerpost. *Got to get out of here. Now.* Real or not, sleeping or waking, she didn't need this. She couldn't, *wouldn't* take it. His slow half-smile was exactly as she'd remembered it. Good God, he *must* be real!

'You're easier to love than you are to forget, silky cat.' Fletch's voice was a husky, caressing whisper in the stillness. The moon glittered in his eyes as he stared up at her.

Moonlight must be harder to breathe than air—thicker. That was why she was so dizzy, her breathing so ragged. She slid one foot backwards, feeling for that top step.

'And if you run, I'll be right behind you, kitten.' It was a gentle, soothing murmur, sounded more promise than threat somehow.

And dizzy as she was, he would catch her, Jolian realised bitterly. 'Damn you, Fletch,' she whispered helplessly. 'You can't keep doing this to me. You can't!'

'Doing what?' he asked tenderly.

'You can't keep stomping back into my life whenever you get the whim. It *hurts* too much ...' The words came out almost a whimper, and she clenched her teeth till her jaws ached.

'You still hurt, silky cat?'

She would not, could not answer that, but her eyes filled slowly with tears. Savagely she brushed them off her lashes.

'Good,' Fletch whispered. His low voice had none of the smoothness she'd remembered, didn't even sound steady. *'Thank God.'* He put a hand on the floor and leaned forward, starting to rise.

Got to get out of here! Jolian snatched at the bannister and half-fell, half-slipped, backwards down one step, her eyes wild.

Fletch froze, his eyes on her face. In the silence she could hear both of them breathing, the moonlight seemed to come and go with the sound. 'Wait,' he murmured at last. It was a soothing, hypnotic sound that went well with the moonlight. Slowly he leaned back against the wall, holding on to her with those glittering eyes, the soothing murmur, 'Please, wait.'

Jolian waited, watching the moonlight ebb and then slowly flow again across the hard planes of his face, waited for her dizziness to pass. He would be stiff from sitting, looked from his pose as if he'd been there a long time. If she was quick, and didn't fall, she might just beat him to the car. Slowly, with her toes, she felt behind her for the next step.

'What have you been doing, this last month?' Fletch asked finally, softly.

'Oh ... working. Having the time of my life,' she answered savagely. 'What about you?' No doubt he'd gone back to his fun and games. All of them.

'Thinking. And nursing Jem and ... thinking ...'

She shouldn't ask. Shouldn't. 'Jem?'

His half-smile was rueful. 'A light case of pneumonia which turned into a whopping case of collegiate mononucleosis. The doctor says he can get out of bed next week ... in time for Thanksgiving.' He moved restlessly, then froze as she flinched and leaned backwards a little. 'It's given us a lot of time for talking,' he added quietly.

Putting a casual foot down on the next step, Jolian shifted her weight towards it, then stopped as his eyebrow slanted up. 'How's Ralph?' she asked quickly.

It hurt to hear his soft laughter. 'In the seventh heaven! Hasn't budged from Jem's pillow all month.'

Keep him distracted—that was the idea—his eyes on her face, not her feet. 'Did Jem ever forgive me?'

'*Forgive* you?' Fletch's crooked smile seemed to hurt his face. 'He misses you, lady ... almost as much as I do ...'

Damn him. Oh, *damn* him. She had to go quickly now. Jolian dragged her toe delicately backwards across the stair tread. 'And your business?' She glanced down to check where she was, gathering her muscles for the spin.

'Sold last week.' The words were flat, but they carried a faint ring of satisfaction, maybe even triumph. He grinned as her widening eyes jerked up to his face.

'Sol——' She stopped, feeling dizzy again. 'But ... so ... what will you do now, Fletch?'

'Build a house.' His low voice was casual, sounded a little smoother now.

'A ... *house*?' Jolian was lost. This wasn't the man she had known. She stepped up one step to peer at him.

He didn't *look* as if he was joking . . .

Fletch nodded. 'It was a dream I used to have . . . to build my own house and all the furniture in it. Jem says he's going to help.'

'Where——' Her voice sounded funny and she swallowed, tried again. 'Where's it going to be, Fletch?'

His eyes gleamed as they stroked slowly across her face. 'We both liked Boston,' he said huskily, 'but we like the country too. Say twenty-five or thirty miles out, in sight of the ocean?'

The questioning note in his voice brought her up the last step. 'And then what will you do, Fletch?'

He smiled slowly, staring up at her with an odd, almost hungry look in those dark eyes. 'Well, I think I'll be a furniture designer when I grow up,' he teased softly.

Her knees were shaking as she crossed the moonlit floor to stand above him. 'And how long do you think that will take, Fletcher McKay?'

His smile vanished. The eyes on her face were unwavering. 'With your help, Jolian? Maybe . . . five years. *Without* it?' His dark head shook faintly, but his eyes never lost her face. 'Maybe never.'

Laughing softly, she reached for his outstretched hand, found it in spite of the silvery, blinding tears. Her body answered the warmth of his lips against her wrist with a blazing surge of joy. By God, he *was* real! '*Fletch!*' Laughing, she leaned back against his hand, tugged gently to bring him to his big feet. 'Come inside.'

Coming Next Month in Harlequin Presents!

743 LEGALLY BOUND Kerry Allyne
She wants a divorce! And as far as she's concerned, there's no chance of reconciliation with her estranged husband. But he won't let her go. And he won't leave her alone.

744 SWEET TEMPEST Helen Bianchin
Appearances can be deceiving. But when a young woman is living with a rakishly handsome vet near Melbourne and pretending to be his lover, there is no mistaking trouble!

745 COMING HOME Alison Fraser
Things get out of hand when an Englishwoman asks a wealthy Greek to accept responsibility for his brother's son. And he thinks she's included in the bargain . . . as his mistress!

746 DARKER SIDE OF DESIRE Penny Jordan
To save the innocent heir to a troubled desert kingdom, two strangers masquerade as the infant's parents. But how long can they disguise their feelings for each other?

747 A NAKED FLAME Charlotte Lamb
Bad publicity fuels the smoldering differences between an actress and her ex-husband on how their son should be raised. It also fans a flame of desire that still burns between them.

748 DOUBLE DOUBTING Jeneth Murrey
A widow becomes stranded at the home of an irresistibly compelling Frenchman. He offers her a chance to feel again. A chance to win—or lose—at love.

749 BOND OF VENGEANCE Jessica Steele
When insult is added to injury, vengeance is called for. Or so an English secretary thinks until she falls in love with her intended victim.

750 VIKING INVADER Sally Wentworth
He is a modern-day conqueror intent on claiming the heart of a fair English maiden. Unfortunately she's already engaged. But that doesn't deter him in the least!

Harlequin Celebrates Thirty-five Years of Excellence

---

6 TOP HARLEQUIN AUTHORS—6 CLASSIC BOOKS!

Join us in celebrating as we reissue six Harlequin novels by some of the best authors in series-romance-publishing history. These books still capture the delight and magic of love as much today as they did when they were originally published by Harlequin. The fact that they transcend time attests to their excellence.

THE 1950s
Nurse/Doctor books—
"delightful books with happy endings."

THE 1960s
An era of "armchair travel" and exotic settings for Harlequin readers

THE 1970s
Harlequin becomes a household word and introduces Harlequin Presents— today, still the most popular series of contemporary romance fiction

THE 1980s
World-renowned authors continue to ensure Harlequin's excellence in romance series publishing

1. GENERAL DUTY NURSE
   by Lucy Agnes Hancock
2. HOSPITAL CORRIDORS
   by Mary Burchell

3. COURT OF THE VEILS
   by Violet Winspear

4. BAY OF NIGHTINGALES
   by Essie Summers
5. LEOPARD IN THE SNOW
   by Anne Mather

6. DAKOTA DREAMIN'
   by Janet Dailey

Introducing
Harlequin Intrigue

Because romance can be quite an adventure.

Available in August wherever paperbacks are sold.

INT-3

BARBARA DELINSKY

Fingerprints

Carly Quinn is a
woman with a past.
Born Robyn Hart, she
was forced to don a new
identity when her intensive
investigation of an arson-ring
resulted in a photographer's death
and threats against her life.

Ryan Cornell's entrance into her life
was a gradual one. The handsome
lawyer's interest was piqued, and then
captivated, by the mysterious Carly — a
woman of soaring passions and a
secret past.